BRIGAND'S BOUNTY

To Sheriff Scott Wagoner it seemed that his Chief Deputy, Jeff Mays, had lost interest in hunting the formidable Yerby gang, but that was not the case. For Mirabelle Drummond's sake, young Jeff was taking a very unorthodox course in fighting the Yerby outfit. Shortly after a stranger had shown a special interest in the Yerby affair, Jeff shocked the Sheriff by handing in his badge. Bullets emptied many saddles, and a few reputations also died in the desperate clashes which took place before Jeff felt justified in wearing a badge again.

Books by David Bingley
in the Linford Western Library:

THE BEAUCLERC BRAND
ROGUE'S REMITTANCE
STOLEN STAR

DAVID BINGLEY

BRIGAND'S BOUNTY

Complete and Unabridged

LINFORD
Leicester

First published in Great Britain in 1969
under the name of 'Bat Jefford'

First Linford Edition
published 2003

British Library CIP Data

Bingley, David, *1920 –*
    Brigand's bounty.—Large print ed.—
Linford western library
1. Western stories
2. Large type books
I. Title
823.9'14 [F]

ISBN 0–7089–9962–X

Published by
F. A. Thorpe (Publishing)
Anstey, Leicestershire

Set by Words & Graphics Ltd.
Anstey, Leicestershire
Printed and bound in Great Britain by
T. J. International Ltd., Padstow, Cornwall

This book is printed on acid-free paper

FOR VERA

1

The two riders with the badges were fifty yards ahead of the other nineteen riders who were trailing hoof dust in a fruitless search of the arid canyon country to the north of Arizona territory. Thirst and frustration showed on the flushed face of the ageing sheriff as he raised his hand and brought the posse to a halt behind him.

'Will you take a look at that heap of crowbait pushers, Jeff?' he requested drily. 'See how quickly they rein their hosses an' let us get ahead? They've no heart for the job. That's their trouble. So help me, it's mine, too.'

Sheriff Scott Wagoner of Waterford County yawned and checked the sweating bay gelding which bore him. The nudge of his knees reminded him of the ache in an old thigh wound. He pressed the place with a gloved hand.

Aware that Jeff Mays' eyes were on him, he turned away towards the rocky, eroded north, half-hidden in heat shimmer, and solemnly mopped his brow.

Wagoner was a stout, grey, balding man of fifty-nine years, rugged of feature and slow moving when out of the saddle. He sported a tall, cream-coloured stetson which made him seem taller than his medium height. Grey stubble on his chin bore witness to a day and a half's endeavour out of town.

The chief deputy was also busy with his bandanna.

Jeff, tall and fair with tapering sideburns, looked older than his twenty-three years as he dabbed his forehead with the red square of cloth. The monotonous riding had peppered his blue shirt and black leather vest with grey dust and laid a grey oval of the same colour on the top of his black stetson.

Jeff glanced back at the other riders before answering.

'I'm jest as weary myself, Scott. I reckon the cinch is wearin' a broad groove round the belly of this buckskin hoss. If he could talk he'd tell how many headlong gallops we'd made into these badland areas in the past year, seekin' out the Yerby outfit, which gets more an' more elusive all the time.'

Wagoner grunted. Together, they swung out of leather and loosened and rocked their saddles. Steam came from under the saddle blankets, testifying to the hard effort made by the horses. One after another, the posse members spilled water into their hats and partially quenched the animals' thirst.

'Do we make for home?' Jeff murmured.

The sheriff made a noise which was hard to describe. He gave a bitter glance at the main group of his men, and reluctantly murmured: 'Yer, I guess I've run out of excuses for goin' forward any more. But that tip from Dwarf Canyon did seem a worthwhile one, though. If the outlaws came this way after shootin' up the two stores I reckon we had our best chance to catch 'em in months.'

'I agree, Scott. But there's always this heat-haze an' the broken ground, too. The terrain helps the lawbreaker an' there's little we can do about it. Maybe one day they'll try an' hold up your office in the county seat. Till then, I guess they've got us on the run.'

'Meanwhile, my term is fast runnin' out an' your reputation continues to take a knock.'

Jeff flinched at this last comment. He was unnecessarily rough with the sweating buckskin as he tightened the saddle strap again. The murmur of conversation grew louder in the larger group as the two leaders were seen to be moving again.

Baldy Peake, the liveryman, screwed up his eyes as he sometimes did over the card table. 'I'd say old Scott is bent on keepin' us out in the open for another day! Any takers?'

Boris Groves, the jailer and junior

deputy, shifted his bandy stance. A sneer appeared on his habitually sour, hollow-cheeked face. He nipped the tuft of black beard on his chin between finger and thumb and nodded towards the isolated pair.

'The sheriff will be out of office in a few weeks, an' Jeff's a careful boy. Who do you think is goin' to toss away his money on a bet like that?'

Although the voices did not carry, Wagoner sent his posse away as though he had overheard their comments and was further angered. He was not heading directly back to Waterford, but making a detour towards the west in order to keep his detractors guessing.

Another hour had gone by, and the sun had shifted quite a way to westward when the first distant dust plume of the converging horse showed itself. Instead of riding harder, the posse slowed, not considering for a moment that this was a member of the scattered Yerby raiders dying to give himself up.

Tired eyes strained through spy-glasses as the speeding figure came nearer. Jeff Mays was the first to identify him.

He drawled: 'Feller's ridin' a black an' white pony — '

'That I can see!' Wagoner cut in.

'Kind of youthful, an' decked out in that fringed buckskin stuff, too. Say, Scott, do you happen to have Turkey on the payroll?'

'*That* young galoot? You ain't tellin' me that's Turkey comin' like a bat out of hell on that pony? He sure must have somethin' motivatin' him, yes, siree!'

Turkey was a youth of about eighteen years. He had been earning his living in one casual way or another around Waterford for over ten years. He was a keen, bright-eyed, cheerful youth, full of curiosity and with a pair of ears that missed nothing. When he was frowning to bunch up his freckles and showing his rather prominent wide-set teeth, usually his wits were at their sharpest.

He rode the pinto like a veteran, and

the long-bladed knife and the .44 Colt at his waist emphasised that he was prepared to give a good account of himself, if trouble came along. Yipping loudly as he came within conversing distance, he walloped the pony with his broad black hat and brought it to a spectacular stop beside the sheriff.

Jeff, also orphaned like the new-comer, backed off because he did not like the way the youngster always put on a show.

The youth and the sheriff exchanged a couple of breathless sentences. Wagoner called: 'Well, Jeff, it ain't like we thought. Seems Turkey, here, ain't found the Yerby gang, but he does have a message an' it's for your ears only!'

Jeff, who was busy with the makings of a cigarette, shot the boy a sharp glance. Turkey dented afresh his big hat and nodded three or four times, pulling his mount away from that of the sheriff.

Jeff hesitated, knowing the eyes of all the posse were upon him. 'It's private, this message?' he probed.

'Absolutely,' Turkey assured him. 'I figure you'll be embarrassed if we don't back off a little.'

At this suggestion, Jeff side-stepped his buckskin until some ten yards separated him from the nearest posse member.

'Now, see here, Turkey, Scott an' me know a lot about the cunnin' little ways you have of makin' a livin' so don't go hopin' too hard that you're goin' to make money out of me!'

'I've been paid,' Turkey remarked cuttingly, 'so don't you trouble yourself none, either.'

With maddening slowness, he unbuttoned the front of his fringed tunic and brought out a buff-coloured packet, swollen with an enclosure which was not paper. He held it out, tentatively. Jeff had to go a little closer to grip it without dropping it.

He pulled off his right riding gauntlet, inserted a finger under the flap and laboriously slit open the top. A single folded sheet of paper was exposed. Deepening curiosity made him forget the other riders and his own mild hostility towards the messenger.

The message was hastily scrawled in pencil:

Jeff Mays,
  Come right away! Pronto!
        M. x

His jaw must have sagged, because Wagoner called across to him.

'Anythin' *I* can do, Jeff? Does it concern county business, or is it personal?'

'It's — it's personal, Sheriff!'

Wagoner and the other twenty listeners heard well, but did not comment. They were all wondering if the message would in any way affect the rest of their day. Jeff's heart thumped. He was surprised that it was not audible above the shifting of horseshoes and the mouthing on bits.

He squeezed the envelope, felt the

bulky object and tipped it into his palm. It almost fell from his hand, he was so surprised at it. All Wagoner noticed was a slight green flash as the sunlight probed something, but Turkey was closer and it took all his self-control for him not to whistle or show his intense excitement in some other way.

The object in question was an earring: wrought in solid silver, it had a big green emerald in the upper part of it and a finely cut diamond on the pendant part, which was suspended on a small chain.

'You aimin' to keep us in suspense indefinitely, Jeff?' Deputy Groves asked, working to keep the edge out of his voice.

'I've got to talk with Scott, here,' Jeff replied brusquely.

'So what have we to say, Jeff?' the senior peace officer mused, when their two horses came together.

'I've got this message, from an old friend. It — it means I've got to ride off, on my own, right now, if you ain't too peevish, Scott? What do you think about it, eh?'

Blunt fingers rasped on the sheriff's chin stubble. He looked annoyed. 'I don't rightly think you ought to be talkin' about me bein' peevish, Jeff. Why, in these past minutes you've shown more spirit than anyone has seen in you for maybe a year. I ain't complainin', but — '

'What you say is true, Scott, but I've still got to go.'

'Well, you ain't after collectin' a bounty all to yourself. I know that much about you, pardner. Can you tell me if you'll be headin' into town?'

Jeff, who was most impatient to be off, shot a quick glance at Turkey, who reluctantly shook his head. Groves moved in closer from behind. He knew that Jeff had pocketed something other than the letter, but he had failed to see what it was.

In his most ingratiating tone, he offered: 'You look kind of excited, Jeff. I'd be glad to ride along with you, if

11

you think you could hit trouble!'

'I might hit trouble if you were with me, Boris. Jest stay away this time, huh?'

The jailer backed off, but not without a lot of frowning and eyebrow-raising for the benefit of the other men. Wagoner signalled his approval with a wave of his hat. A minute later, Jeff and the messenger had gone off in a cloud of dust which had the sheriff coughing again.

Another punishing hour of riding across broken country to the south showed Jeff that they were headed for some place west of the county seat. When he was sure of this, he reined in and insisted on Turkey telling him more.

'Now is the time to talk, Turkey. Are you supposed to take me all the way to this rendezvous?'

'I ain't supposed to tell you, leastways, not yet!'

The youth had thrust out his full underlip and was gazing into the distance, between his pony's ears.

'Come on, that ain't the way to behave when a peace officer questions you! You know this is troubled territory! How do I know you ain't leadin' me into a trap set up by one of those Yerby boys?'

Turkey flushed, but he gave his attention. 'I know you're bluffin', Jeff, but I'll tell you what you want to know. You're to ride to Two Mile Rock, then use the bear track which runs north-west from there. Along the track, not too far, you'll make contact! That's all I know.'

'I've heard you an' I'm askin' you one more thing. Who did you get the envelope from?'

Jeff's blue eyes looked formidable as they studied Turkey's troubled countenance.

'It was a young feller with brown hair. Not a face I knew, or would remember.'

Turkey spoke finally. Without warning, he turned his mount and sent it off in a new direction. Jeff took a few deep breaths to relax him before setting off at a cracking pace for Two Mile Rock.

Two Mile Rock was about two miles west of Waterford. It reared up in the middle of the trail like a bent and beckoning finger to a height of about fifteen feet. Everyone in the neighbourhood knew it. Jeff cut down on the distance to it with his thoughts on the coming encounter.

The 'M' on his letter was Mirabelle. Several years back they had been like brother and sister in the same household over the border in Colorado State. Jeff's parents, like so many others in the West, had died young. His mother's brother, the Reverend Robert Jones, had taken him in and finished off the job of seeing him through his most youthful and critical years.

Mirabelle, the reverend's daughter, was the only other member of the household. She had been more like an older sister than a cousin to Jeff. The latter had cut himself off from his kin in his late teens when he insisted on riding away from their home in Gorge City, Colorado, to seek his fortune.

Jeff had never been back to see them. In the meantime, the parson had died, but his daughter was alive and well. This message by Turkey proved that. Around twelve months earlier, Jeff had happened upon Mirabelle, dressed in a man's trail garb and in charge of a lightweight covered wagon in the county seat.

He had been overjoyed to see her, but her anxious mien and the way she talked had quickly calmed his feelings. In answer to his questions she had tried to make it clear that she was no longer unattached, and that she was well cared for. She had stopped him enquiring as to where her home was located, and also prevented him from examining too closely the contents of the wagon.

The meeting came at a time when Jeff was new to his badge. He would have liked a word of commendation from her for the useful job he was attempting to do. But all Mirabelle seemed to want was to get as far away from him as possible in the least possible time.

There had been strain in the way she talked, and dark smudges under her eyes which suggested that she did not sleep well. He remembered her as he had last seen her, in a man's white shirt, black denims, and wearing her long, dark brown hair in a big coil over one shoulder. Only one of her ears showed, and dangling from that was the flashing earring and pendant which now reposed in an envelope in his shirt pocket.

Their last words together came drifting back into his mind.

'If that's the way you want it, Mirabelle, I won't ask any more questions. I'll let you ride out of my life again the way you rode in. You know where I am, an' what my job is. If you ever want anythin' — '

'I'll send you a message an' you'll

come a-ridin' real fast, Jeff!'

Her long-fingered gentle hand had rested on his arm when she said this, and he knew that he would never be able to refuse whatever she asked of him. In the past twelve months he had often mused over whether she would send for him. He had made up his mind that there was something in her life that she did not want the law to know too much about.

It was this consideration which curbed his ardour to fight the Yerby gang and make a personal issue of it. He knew that Mirabelle had driven her wagon into the western end of the canyon country which the posses were so frequently scouring for renegades. He felt that if he became too deeply involved in the chasing he might, quite by chance, foul up the life of the young woman to whom he owed most in life.

Receiving the message in the way he had had shocked him. He had proof that the girl was still in the undesirable area. And now she wanted help. He wondered if the kind of help she wanted would affect his conscience as a peace officer: if his future with the county sheriff's office would be compromised.

2

Two Mile Rock came and went. The buckskin's steaming hide, its drooping neck and slightly shorter stride were a better guide to the effort of man and horse than the passage of time. The going, over the beginnings of the bear track, was upgrade and punishing to an animal which had made such a sustained effort.

A furlong up the new route Jeff first got the idea that he had another rider at his back. The shrubs were thick, green and high, and backed by scrub pine, which went a long way towards masking the movements of a pursuer. The buckskin noted the new presence, but it was too tired to do anything about it, other than a certain kind of whinny and a shaking of the muzzle.

Jeff turned about in the saddle. He kept that way for several hundred yards.

In that time, he confirmed that he had company, but not the type of rider. He coaxed his tired mind to think over all the implications of Mirabelle and her secret life. He decided that whoever was behind him should not be there. Besides, a pursuer — in these lonely parts — following a man with a badge, might be intent upon his destruction.

He decided to be rid of the fellow, whoever he was, without losing valuable time. A quick swivelling in leather put him back to facing the way ahead. His plan evolved when they passed under a bent outcrop, flanking the broadening track on the north side. This was the place to make his move.

Having passed it, he increased his pace, pulling up a hundred yards or more beyond. Screened by two pines, he slipped to the ground, unsheathed his Winchester and carefully applied it to his shoulder. Faint sounds marked the pursuer's approach to the outcrop. He studied the face of the rock and tensed himself for the effort of rigidity.

Bushes stirred as the rider reached the critical spot. Jeff squeezed the trigger. He fired, levered and fired again, shooting off four bullets in all. Each of them ripped into the side of the outcrop and was deflected misshapenly across the line of ride of the pursuer.

The horse, which might have been two-coloured, snickered in alarm and threw up its forelegs. The rider echoed its fear and promptly launched himself out of the saddle on the opposite side, arms and legs well spread, like a leaping frog.

No bullets came from the pursuer, and yet Jeff felt that the other fellow was not seriously injured. The pinto disappeared from view, reappeared tossing its head and neck, and showed beyond doubt that its reins were snagged on something.

This was all the deputy wanted to know at this stage. He wiped down the buckskin with handfuls of grass, sprang back into leather and rode on again. The animal was a fast quarter-miler, but on this day of days a fast quarter-mile was beyond it.

Jeff's neck hairs were still prickling when the voice called to him.

'Howdy, Jeff, you made it real soon. You must be tired.'

Mirabelle stepped clear of a tree trunk on the west side of the track. She was tall for a woman, around five feet seven inches. Her expression was much the same as he had always remembered it. The green eyes, the high cheekbones and delicate features were all the same, but the full, generous mouth appeared to be set a little firmer and there were definite smudges under the eyes.

For a few moments, he was too enthralled to answer. He noted that the lush head of brown hair was entirely hidden under the flat-topped dun hat. No wonder Turkey had described her as a young man with brown hair. The gentle curve of breast gave her away under Jeff's close scrutiny. No man's chest could rise and fall in that way.

'Did you have trouble back there?'

Mirabelle went on.

'Yes, somebody was trailin' me. I've spent long enough ridin' after trouble in these parts to want to discourage a pursuer. But how about you? You have some special problem?'

'I said I wouldn't send for you unless I had.' She whistled quietly and a spritely grey mare came up out of a hollow where it had been cropping grass. 'This is an emergency, all right. I don't know if you'll want to do as I ask.'

'Try me, Mirabelle.'

Fighting off the feeling of foreboding which was building up inside him, Jeff slipped to the ground. He put his arms round the girl and kissed her lightly on both cheeks. Mirabelle shuddered, and managed to relax a little. The earring went into her pocket unnoticed.

'Do we have to go some other place?'

She nodded, gently disengaged herself, and mounted the mare. Jeff forked leather again and waited for her to lead. The mare's fine example gave the buckskin a new lease of energy. As more miles slipped by beneath them, Mirabelle's talk took the whole of Jeff's attention.

'Jeff, my husband is dying. No, I'm not wantin' you to try an' patch him up. He's past that. You see, he's spent a lot of his time recently breakin' in hosses. Today he tangled with one that got the better of him. He's badly broken up. His ribs have fouled his lungs, an' maybe his heart, too.'

The girl paused, glanced at her companion and divined his thoughts.

She sounded rather bitter when she resumed. 'Jeff, you don't bring ordinary doctors to Ben Yerby. Except at pistol point, an' I couldn't do that. There are other considerations, too. In showing a doctor where Ben lies, I could be bringin' a whole lot more trouble to myself, an' he wouldn't want that. Besides, medical men don't hurry to wanted outlaws.'

Jeff sighed. 'Mirabelle, I don't know what to make of all this. You know me for a lawman. Lawmen only dash to outlaws to try an' arrest them! Why, I've ridden miles in the last day tryin' to locate the outfit which carries your husband's name! What can you expect of me?'

A short silence built up between them.

'You weren't terribly surprised when I said jest now I was Ben Yerby's wife?'

'Nope. I more or less figured somethin' like that had happened, after the way you acted the last time we met. As a matter of fact, I've been kind of holdin' back lately, in case I ran myself head on into trouble an' found you at the end of it.'

'So you still care for the cousin who acted as a sister to you, Jeff,' the girl murmured, with a brief smile.

'You're about the only person I'm truly obliged to in the world. An' you know it. Otherwise I wouldn't be here. But I'm still puzzled. You must have changed if you could marry this renegade an' stay married to him, knowin' full well who he was an' the way he behaved!'

'Jeff, I'll try to explain to you later. Believe me when I say it's Ben who's changed. He wants you to do him a favour, on account of me. I couldn't bring myself to ask you in so many words. I want you to hurry, an' if you can, do as he says. If you don't hurry he'll be dead, an' then you'll have had the ride for nothin'.'

'I don't follow that last argument, Mirabelle. If your man dies, you'll want someone to look after you, an' I'm here. Are you tellin' me there's somebody else?'

'No. Nobody else, other than you, Jeff. Now, will you ride on alone an' see Ben? He's about three hundred yards farther on, in timber shade by the east side of the track. Me, I'm cuttin' off into the next valley. If you want to see me again, you'll find me in a small ranch house beyond a timber stand in the direction of Bitter Spring Creek.'

'I take it you'd like me to come alone?'

'Please, Jeff. I want to make a complete break with this part of the territory. But mark my words, if you come, it could be dangerous for you.'

The deputy had wanted to ask if there was any danger of his riding into an ambush, but somehow he managed to avoid the question. He touched his hat, swung the buckskin well clear and began to cut down on the distance to the fallen man.

The mare remained almost motionless until he had travelled some fifty yards. Hearing it prance off again, Jeff glanced back. He saw that she had found the earring. It was in position on her right ear lobe. She waved and broke trail to westward. Jeff waved back, almost too late, as the widespread scrub absorbed her.

Minutes later, he saw a big dusty boot sticking out from small rocks. A croaking voice called him over. All six feet of Ben Yerby was stretched out along the ground. He was on his back with his big head resting on his hat.

'Howdy, Deputy. Will you come close? We got things to say to each other an' I'm short on time.'

Jeff nodded. He dismounted without ever taking his eyes off the fallen man.

'You seen Mirabelle?'

The pearl-handled revolvers were still in the renegade's holsters. Jeff supposed that even this near to death he might manage to use one, if he felt deeply enough about it. He nodded from two yards away, squatting on his haunches.

'What sort of a favour do you expect to get out of me, a deputy sheriff?'

The barred brows and deepset eyes matched the picture of the outlaw on the reward notice, along with the bent nose; but Yerby was heavier than the photograph had shown. He had also grown a heavy black moustache which transformed his appearance to some extent.

'I want you to shoot me dead, take my corpse, an' collect the reward money for my widow!'

Yerby winced and lowered his head to bite back pain, at a time when he really needed to study the newcomer's face.

Oddly enough, it was Jeff who groaned. 'I can take her away an' look after her without any of your blood money, Yerby.'

'Sure, sure, I know you can, but won't you do this one little thing for me, on account of the girl? She's suffered this past year or so. I want her to have a few creature comforts when I'm gone. Will you do it, Deputy?'

The effort of trying to persuade his reluctant helper made him cough. Blood trickled from the side of his mouth. Jeff knew he was going to do what was asked of him, even though reward collecting was totally against his nature and beliefs. Even so, he found it hard to say anything which would afford the dying man relief.

'That earring she wears. Was it part of the proceeds of a robbery?'

'It belonged to my mother. You know

29

Mirabelle. She wouldn't have those kinds of gifts!'

The outlaw's eyes rolled, but he held on, seeing Jeff indistinctly. Jeff, for his part, was surprised at his own toughness in such a situation. He found it hard to forget all the fruitless hours spent in scouring the unwholesome canyon country for killers and robbers who were supposed to make up this man's gang.

'You're askin' a lot of a peace officer, Yerby. Tell me somethin' that will help in the fight against your outfit, an' I might help you now!'

Yerby nodded very carefully. 'Keep an eye on Studley. You get that? Studley!'

He raised a hand to his neck and drew one finger across his throat, as though miming a noose around his neck. He wanted to say more, but this time he was too weak. He foamed at the mouth again, lost control of his neck muscles, and barely succeeded in pointing to his heart. Life had just ebbed when the two bullets from Jeff's Colt ripped into the heart, throwing the body about for a few seconds.

The tired buckskin, cropping a few yards away, threw back its head and backed off a few feet. Jeff pushed his hat down the back of his neck and allowed the faint breeze to caress his scalp.

Although he did not know for certain if he was the true cause of Yerby's death, he was committed now. He bent over the body, lifted the twin guns from the holsters and fired three shots out of each down trail towards the south.

They were still smoking when he replaced them. For a minute or so, he blushed unseen over the lies he would have to tell to make this killing story stand up.

3

For a few minutes, the deputy's brain refused to function. All he could do was roll a smoke and slake his thirst. He became aware that his stomach was flapping with emptiness, and that he had not eaten since breakfast. He was not the type of man to do his best work while hungry.

He built a small fire and set his coffee pot over it. While the water heated he searched for the animal on which Yerby must have arrived. To his surprise he found it pegged out about seventy yards away. He could only think that Mirabelle must have done it. It was a sinewy black stallion with a wild look in its eyes.

He won its interest with the offer of water, and after a short sharp struggle, he managed to fork it and take control. His meal of coffee, biscuits and bacon was taken standing up. Ben Yerby's dead weight posed another problem, but after a ten-minute struggle he managed to drape the body over the buckskin, which objected to being staked out for loading.

The scratch meal and the excess energy in the skittery black stallion did a lot towards replenishing Jeff's stamina. With the buckskin in tow, he backtracked to the place where Mirabelle had broken with the track, and cautiously moved west over dry ground and small loose boulders.

He had a feeling that although he had done exactly what Yerby had asked him to do, things would never be the same between Mirabelle and him. How could a woman feel any affection for the man who had helped make her a widow? Not a woman like Mirabelle, anyway.

His spirits were low when he topped a low scrub-covered rise and saw the first gentle undulations of the swale, liberally strewn with bunch grass which was yellow at the top and green lower down. Along the lowest line of the valley was a promising track which led unerringly towards timber, and farther on, towards the rather slow-moving and remote waterway which had won the name Bitter Spring Creek.

Mirabelle awaited him, hatless, in the shade of the timber stand. She held a hand to her heart as her gaze went beyond the rider to the slack corpse on the tired buckskin.

'Don't spend a lot of time lookin' over him, sis,' Jeff begged, using an old familiar term of endearment. 'I've done as he asked me, an' I came along here because there's maybe things I have to do for the livin' before I take his body in to show it to the authorities.'

Walking at the black's head, the girl looked baffled.

'I'm thinkin' of you, sis. You ain't goin' to tell me you were Mrs Yerby an' your man never had any dealings with other outlaws. Hasn't it occurred to you that you may be in some danger?'

Mirabelle anxiously nibbled her

thumb. 'You could be right, Jeff. There's no outlaws around the ranch now, but we never could be sure jest when they'd turn up, an' none of them ever really trusted me. I was too straightforward for them. Only Ben kept them offen me, although they didn't have a lot of time for him this last year or so.'

'How come they felt like that about him?' Jeff asked.

'Oh, he's been wantin' out of the renegade business ever since we married, Jeff. He'd have made it, too, only some of his associates pulled him back into the business.'

'Was he in Dwarf Canyon lately?'

'If you mean was he there to carry out a raid, the answer is no. 'Cause he ain't taken part in a raid since we settled in these parts. All he's done is break a few useful ponies for others, an' grudgingly give them food an' lodgin' when they forced themselves upon us.'

Jeff's expression showed that this

35

statement was hard to believe.

'That's the way it's been, an' I wouldn't lie to you, Jeff. Oh, they used his name all right, still callin' the outfit the Yerby gang. But Ben ain't been with them. I managed to change him a little, you see. Not bein' able to break completely with the gang made him rather a bitter person these past few months.'

They hitched the two horses to the rail outside the house, which was closely ringed by a bunkhouse, a cook shack, a stable and a barn. Jeff stumbled over a litter of wheels and saddlery as he stamped up on to the gallery in search of the coffee which Mirabelle had prepared.

She made a workmanlike job of grooming the buckskin, while Jeff demolished half a fruit pie with his drink. All the time she kept her face averted from the slumped body of her husband, propped on the steps.

The meal finished, Jeff prowled the establishment. He found signs that others had been around recently. When questioned, Mirabelle explained that she had sent old Smithy, the cook, and Dan, a crippled boy, away from the ranch while there was no one to stop them. They had left without question when they knew the mistress was leaving, and Jeff saw no reason to go after them.

'Go pack a bag, sis, an' hurry over it. I've got to find you a new base before any of those outlaw jaspers come a-ridin' this way.'

The look on his face confirmed that he expected company at any time. Mirabelle worked fast, in spite of the way her emotions were churning over inside her. She packed a carpet bag with clothes and a few valuables and scrambled into the saddle of the mare inside fifteen minutes.

'Anythin' you've forgotten?' Jeff queried.

Keeping her lips tightly closed, Mirabelle shook her head. They headed down valley and farther west again: two horses, a mare, a man, a woman and a corpse.

The hideout where Jeff established Mirabelle an hour later was a dugout with a sod roof and three earth walls. It was a comedown for a young woman of some breeding who had been more or less her own mistress, but she accepted the inconvenience of the place, knowing that Jeff was placing her safety above her comfort, for a short while.

Each of them believed that she might be in some danger from the rest of the Yerby outfit, but they did not discuss it. Jeff was anxious to move away again with the body, so as not to lead anyone to his cousin. He was also nervous about the coming confrontations in town.

For the time it took to smoke a cigarette, he sat his buckskin and talked with her.

'Am I right in thinkin' you'll still be ridin' against the Yerby gang, Jeff?'

'Now that your man is out of the way, I can't see any reason why I shouldn't. They've terrorised this county for far too long, an' I'll be makin' it my special business to hunt them into the ground. That's one reason why they shouldn't find you, or know that we are kin. Understand?'

She nodded. 'You want I should tell you the names of men in the gang?'

In any other circumstances Jeff would have answered in the affirmative. In this case, he shook his head. 'In the event the outlaws find you, it's better you say truthfully you didn't give them away.'

The girl edged forward and laid a hand on his knee. 'Shucks, Jeff, it sure is good to know a girl isn't wholly on her own. Thanks for thinkin' about me. I hope you make out all right with what Ben asked you to do.'

'So do I.' Jeff sounded rather bitter. He forced a smile so as not to upset Mirabelle. 'Ben gave me a lead. He mentioned Studley before he died.'

'I'm glad he wanted to help you.'

Jeff blustered. He bent down and kissed his cousin on the cheek. He untethered the buckskin and the black and began his return to town.

The sad parting from his only kin was well to the back of his mind when the plodding stallion carried him into the west end of Waterford about two hours before sundown. The first glimpse of the body whipped the strolling townsfolk into action. Soon they were shouting from one sidewalk to the other and running up the dirt of the road surface for a closer view of the head and features.

Jeff smoked and nodded, but failed to answer the countless queries as to who the stiff was and how he had come by the body. He kept his shoulders hunched and pretended that he was a whole lot more fatigued than he really was. His first stop was by the hitchrail outside the sheriff's office.

He slipped easily to the ground, slackened the saddle girths and was about to hurry indoors, but a couple of burly townsmen with fixed grins on their faces stood in his way.

40

'Hell an' tarnation, Jeff, we can see how tired you are, but you could at least tell us who it is!' one man remonstrated.

'All right, amigo, if you must know, it's Ben Yerby. Now, if it's all the same to you, I've got to report to my superior!'

They moved out of his way, then, repeating the name of the dead outlaw and calling that Wagoner was elsewhere. Jeff shrugged and entered the office. He found it empty. He slumped into the swivel chair, located Scott's whisky bottle in a bottom drawer, and gave himself a big mouthful of it.

Next he rolled a fat smoke and lit it from the last matchstick in his hat band. There was a wash basin in a corner. He filled it from the ewer and bathed his head, neck, hands and arms. His shirt was about to come off when he heard a sharp argument developing on the street.

'I don't believe that's Ben Yerby, an' if it is, Jeff Mays didn't kill him,'

Deputy Groves was saying. His voice was slightly slurred, as though he had been washing away the rigours of the day with strong liquor.

'Well, somebody did, Boris,' a voice challenged, ''cause he sure does look like a straight case of lead poisonin' to me!'

Groves thought that one over. 'If he's shot the bullets will be in the back!' he remarked tersely.

'You mean Jeff shot him in the back,' a distant voice corrected.

At once some six or seven observant men, who could clearly see the back of Yerby's trunk, argued that such was not the case. The argument was at its loudest when Jeff threw open the office door and pushed his way to the rail.

He stuck his thumbs in his belt, and nodded: 'These gents are right, Boris. You want to take back the suggestion I shot Ben Yerby Drummond in the back?'

Groves was shaking his head and bestowing a sneering laugh on all and sundry before Jeff had finished speaking. 'You may be the chief deputy round here, Jeff, but you don't scare me! You ain't scared anybody in a whole year, an' that's the truth!'

Jeff reached forward, grabbed his detractor, and held him by the bandanna while his head rattled against a post. Groves' grey hat left his head and cartwheeled into the dirt.

'There's been a change, Boris, an' you're goin' to see positive proof of it! You have a big mouth, an' a loose tongue an' I'm all for doin' somethin' about it, so defend yourself!'

The jailer's neck was released, and a couple of seconds later a swift right swing landed on the side of his jaw, banging his head against the post once again. His lower jaw went slack, but he recovered, bending at the waist and catfooting away sideways, nearer to the wall.

Jeff, following up closely, narrowly avoided a bench with his knee. Groves countered with a vicious left swing, aimed for the body. It could have been a telling blow, except that it landed flush on Jeff's belt buckle and skinned the knuckles. After that, Groves scored once or twice to the chest and high on the angle of the jaw, but Jeff was scarcely feeling the weight of the punches.

He spent a minute or two learning how to sway away from them or duck under. Then, as his legs began to tire after the day's protracted riding, he went over to the attack again, and was soon scoring fairly freely. Groves began to gasp every time a punch landed. The end was in sight when Jeff landed twice on the point of the bearded chin, but the punch which sent Groves down for the count was a haymaking right hook which landed on the side of his neck.

Jeff rested his legs on the rail until he had recovered his breath. Groves stayed still. The winner was still angered enough to haul him along with ease and dump him in the nearest trough.

Sheriff Wagoner came through the

crowd from an eating house just as the waves began to subside, and the excited onlookers were drying themselves off.

'Seems to me, Jeff, as if you're makin' a grandstand return! I don't rightly cotton on to my chief deputy dowsin' the jailer near my office, though. Maybe you ought to come inside an' explain!'

Jeff shrugged and shook his head. 'I'm too tired to explain right now, Scott. The fact is, I'm jest goin' along to Slim Baron's to have Ben Yerby measured for a box! Would you care to come along with him?'

Wagoner made a great play of dusting off his big hat. He hoped that Jeff's words had not carried to many of the onlookers. As soon as he had satisfied himself that the corpse was that of Yerby, he fell into step beside his assistant and did not utter another word until the undertaker's office was reached.

Slim Baron, the undertaker, a man of advancing years with a huge waistline, was on the floor above enjoying to the last morsel his evening meal.

Between them, the two peace officers carried in the body and laid it on the usual measuring slab in the back room. Scott Wagoner leaned across it with the air of a conspirator.

'Tell me how it happened, Jeff! You had this tip off — an' you located Yerby more or less where the message said . . . You had a shoot out with him an' got your bullets in first?'

'Somethin' like that, Scott, only I'm kind of still tense an' I'd rather not talk about it, if you don't mind. He was on his own when I found him, an' I certainly put them bullets in his body, so help me!'

The sheriff drummed a tune with his fingers on the table. 'One thing I'm real curious about, Jeff, an' that is the hombre who tipped you off. Would you care to tell me about him?'

'No, I wouldn't,' Jeff returned flatly. 'Why don't you mosey around town an' ask Turkey. He sure enough has the loosest tongue, maybe exceptin' Boris Groves.'

'I'm aimin' to ask Turkey, Jeff,' Wagoner returned mildly, 'only he ain't around to ask right now.'

Jeff went suddenly thoughtful. His mind went back to the rider who had pursued him towards the meeting place with Mirabelle. He had intended to look around the place on the way back, but the developments over Yerby had made him forget. Now, he was starting to wonder if Turkey had been his pursuer and, if he had been, whether those ricochets had gone too close and done him any serious damage.

Jeff found it was not easy to shrug off the matter. He did not sound at all confident when he answered.

'You an' I know jest how much Turkey gets around, Scott. He'll turn up when he's good an' ready. I don't figure he'll have a lot to tell you, though.'

A creeping on the inner stairs suggested that Slim was on his way to deal with them. He came through the stairs door breathing hard as usual and started to congratulate Jeff on his achievement. The latter backed off and gave over the exchanges to the sheriff. Wagoner coaxed Baron into making the measurements, and asked him to fetch the doctor to make out a death certificate before the light faded too much.

Baron assured them of his full co-operation, and they left. Farther down the street, there was a lamp shining in the private office of Tom Thomasson, a lawyer empowered by Wells, Fargo and other large companies to deal with the payment of rewards.

Wagoner collided with Jeff, who stopped outside. 'On the ride in, Scott, I've changed a great many of my ideas. I'm figurin' on collectin' every penny of the reward money due for bringing in Ben Yerby. I'd take it kindly if you'd step in here with me an' assure the lawyer that Ben really is the fellow ready for plantin'!'

Wagoner whistled, but signified that he was willing to give evidence for the reward. One behind the other, they went indoors. Thomasson kept them a full half hour. Jeff was still leading the way when they emerged again. His face showed his quiet elation as he strode off to his bed in the building behind the courthouse.

He paused at the corner. 'Oh, Scott, would you like me to try an' breathe some life into that jailer of yours before I turn in?'

Scott shook his head and let the ribbing ride. In the office, Groves, who was touching up the bruises on his face, caught the full force of the sheriff's displeasure and took himself out of the older man's presence at the first opportunity.

Left on his own, Wagoner produced an old tobacco pipe. He only smoked it when he was in a very thoughtful mood.

'Jeff,' he murmured, to the empty room, 'you've changed again, boy.

You're actin' like you were a whole twelvemonth ago, when I entertained the hope that Waterford County might be cleaned out of outlaws. I wonder if this present mood will hold?'

4

Sheriff Wagoner was restless after Jeff had gone to his quarters. He emptied the lowest drawer of his desk, and leafed through the reward notices in there, as recent events had driven the idea of sleep from his mind. He had paced for ten minutes with an empty pipe in his mouth when a faint knock at the office door broke in upon his reverie.

'Come in, it's open!' he barked.

He stood with his weight evenly balanced until the man who had knocked moved indoors. It was Tom Thomasson, the lawyer. Thomasson was a slim, quickmoving man of average height, in his middle fifties. He wore a round-brimmed black hat, a tailored coat of the same colour and neat dark trousers and boots. A fringe of curling white hair stood out from under the hat behind his temples and at the nape of his neck. In contrast, the arched brows and thin moustache were jet black in colour. He surveyed the sheriff with round, alert grey eyes and a thin cigar moved up and down at the corner of his mouth.

'You busy, Scott?'

'Only with my thoughts, Tom. Take a seat, won't you? Sure was interestin', that little meetin' of ours a few minutes ago.'

Thomasson dusted off an upright chair and straddled it. 'I couldn't help bein' interested the way things were, Scott. Is Jeff around?'

The sheriff explained that his deputy had turned in for the night, and the lawyer felt emboldened to speak freely. 'I don't know how you thought about the revelations, Scott. It seemed to me that Jeff was actin' mighty circumspect. Kind of aggressive in his manner, too.'

'I'll say this, Tom,' the sheriff replied, pointing with his pipe stem, 'if Jeff had been givin' evidence in court, instead of talkin' privately in your office, he'd have had to speak a whole lot more frankly, or upset the judge!'

Thomasson nodded. 'I suppose the way he sees it, we ought to be good and thankful we have Yerby ready for plantin'. Us an' a lot of other folk, too. That outfit has been a darned nuisance in this county an' the neighbourin' territories for quite a long time. Must be ten years or more since I first heard the name of Yerby. I find it hard to believe the fellow is really dead, an' that a man from this town took him single-handed. Did Jeff say any more about how it came about? After he left my office, I mean?'

Scott tossed the Yerby reward notice across. Thomasson noted that it was three years old, and that when the picture was printed the wanted man had no moustache.

'No, Tom, he didn't say much. It wasn't like him, really. We were like strangers. He acted as though I had no right to question him. I'm glad Yerby is out of the reckonin' but I don't altogether like what's happened to Jeff.'

'I can see what you mean, Scott. He's gone all tough again, an' we've grown used to havin' him the other way. One thing I felt would never happen, though, an' that was to have Jeff come along an' claim a reward. We've seen him change while he's worked out of your office, but I never thought to hear him say different about rewards. That's the mysterious thing, from my point of view.'

Thomasson stayed long enough to smoke a fresh cigar before he left. His conversation helped to settle the disturbed sheriff, but the discussion did nothing further to enlighten them as to how the chief deputy had made his private killing. As they stood before the open door prior to parting, the lawyer made sure that they were not overheard and then asked a last question.

'There's no doubt he'll get the reward, in full, but have you any idea what he'll spend it on, Scott?'

'Land's sakes, Tom, I don't have the faintest idea. If he's got any sort of private life, I don't know about it. I don't know anybody who does know about it, either.'

They parted in a friendly fashion. The lawyer went off to his rooms and Wagoner remained standing in the office doorway, fumbling more tobacco into the bowl of his pipe.

A half hour before dusk, a sorry figure entered town at the west end of Main Street. The man, hunched forward on the back of a limping horse, managed to slide to the ground and stay upright when the horse halted outside the livery.

Baldy Peake, the owner of the stable, who was busily playing patience in his dusty office with a lamp swinging low and bright above his head, looked up in surprise and identified the newcomer through the window. Peake stifled a startled exclamation and hurried out of doors.

'Turkey? What in tarnation is the

matter with you? You looked as if you'd barely survived a brush with Injuns!'

The youth managed a faint grin, but he had obviously been badly shaken during his protracted ride out of town. 'Well, I'll allow the posse got back to town a couple of minutes before I did, but why are we waitin' out here?'

There was a grumbling tone in the young man's voice which he found hard to disguise. Peake took the reins and Turkey's right arm. He was about to lead both of them in through the wide door when he spotted a trace of blood down the lad's left sleeve.

'Hey, you *have* been in trouble! You want I should call the Doc?'

'No, I don't think that will be necessary, Baldy. Jest give me a hand to patch myself up is all I ask. I ain't lookin' for publicity this trip!'

There was a sofa with a sprout or two of horsehair coming out of it in the dining office. Peake made Turkey stretch out on it and take off his coat. The livery was one of the places where the young man regularly made his quarters free of charge. The owner thought nothing of making use of his office on this occasion.

'That's a bullet groove,' Peake remarked tersely, as he spotted the red furrow down the back of Turkey's left upper arm.

'I've got another one, a bit fainter, across my right hip, if you want to investigate further.'

'I'll go get me a bucket of water an' some clean cloths,' Peake suggested.

While he was out of the office, he took a quick look at the pinto and found that it had picked up a pebble. The stone was lodged in one of the front shoes. Probably Turkey had felt too tired to pick it out with his knife. The pinto could have been in much worse shape.

Ten minutes later, the buckskin outfit had been discarded. Peake had doctored both bullet grooves and patched them up. The unaccustomed form of exercise had left him rather breathless.

He looked to Turkey to enlighten him, but his patient was uncharacteristically quiet and seemingly distracted.

'Now, see here, Turkey, you're actin' as though you had done somethin' seriously wrong. I don't figure that's the case. Even if it is you don't have to hold anythin' back from me. Why, I'm old enough to be your Pa an' then some!'

'If you want to be fatherly to me, Baldy,' Turkey murmured, 'you've got to take this little lot on trust. I ain't sayin' what happened to me after I left you with the sheriff an' the rest of the posse!'

'But Jeff Mays was with you when you left the rest of us, boy. Did you collect these grooves after Jeff had parted company with you?'

Turkey set his jaw hard, and instead of getting an answer, Peake felt bound to mumble an apology for his further questioning. He did what he could then to make a scratch meal for the youth, and helped him up the ladder into the hayloft with it. One of Turkey's peculiarities was that he liked to eat alone.

Peake took the pebble from under the pinto's plate, and inspected the other animals left in his care. Jeff Mays' buckskin and Yerby's black stallion, brought in by one of Slim Baron's men, both looked tired. In fact, they were stretched out in the straw and no longer interested in anything that could happen that day.

Peake shook his head over them. He finished his chores, pulled on a shabby vest and his hat, and paused at the foot of the ladder.

'Turkey, I'm goin' to look me out a bit of company. Is there anythin' I can get for you?'

'No, Baldy. Not right now. Nothin' at all. Adios.'

The liveryman shrugged and left.

* * *

But for the cloud of smoke from the silent man's tobacco pipe, Baldy Peake

59

would have barged right into Sheriff
Wagoner in the doorway of his office.

'Doggone it, Baldy, this sure is a
long, busy day. Come on inside, won't
you? I don't figure you've come all the
way along the street at this time of day
simply to discuss the price of hoss-
shoeing nails!'

Peake was perturbed by what he had
come to discuss, but he managed to
raise a chuckle while Wagoner put a
match to a main lamp and lowered it
over the desk. The liveryman was slow
to come to the point, but when he did,
he spoke rapidly.

'Turkey is back. He's got a couple of
bullet grooves an' I'm kind of worried
about him, but he won't say anythin' to
me, at all, as to how he came by them.
On top of that, his pony had picked up
a stone an' he didn't appear to have the
strength to get it out himself.'

Wagoner nodded several times, his
eyes much brighter since the news. He
coughed and held back his reply.

'I was thinkin', Scott . . . '

'What was you thinkin', amigo?'

'Well, Turkey took Jeff away from the posse, an' Jeff was the one who came back alone with the outlaw's corpse. Do you think them bullet grooves could have been made by Yerby's guns, or the guns of some of his boys?'

Wagoner thought over the possibility. He started to shake his head without quite knowing why. 'It's a possibility, but I don't think so. For two reasons. One, I don't think Jeff would have taken along a boy as raw as Turkey is, if he knew he was headin' for a gun showdown with Ben Yerby.'

The sheriff dried up and became very thoughtful. He had to be prompted to give his second reason. He shook his head like a sleeper freshly awakened.

'The other reason? Oh, that's easy. I don't think Yerby, or any of his boys, would have been satisfied to leave Turkey alive with jest a couple of scratches. Do you?'

Peake found himself agreeing, but in accepting the sheriff's reasoning, he was no nearer knowing exactly what had happened.

'But who did it, then? Who would want to shoot a callow youth like Turkey?'

Wagoner called upon many years' experience in giving his views on the big question. 'I'd say it was somebody who didn't know him at all, or, failin' that, a man who knew him but didn't know he was shootin' at him.'

Peake gaped at him. The liveryman's grey matter was not as good as that of the peace officer. Wagoner massaged his weak hip before entering upon his explanation.

'Turkey is a mighty curious boy, ain't he, Baldy?'

This query raised an affirmative nod.

'Assumin' Jeff dismissed him when he knew where to ride, can you imagine Turkey swallowin' all his curiosity an' ridin' for home without seekin' to find out anythin' more about the meetin'?'

At last Peake began to see an explanation. 'But do you think Jeff would be justified in nickin' the boy like that?' His voice was hushed.

'He didn't have to know it was a boy. He might have thought it was an outlaw. Remember, he was in outlaw country.'

Peake obviously believed that Jeff had shot the youth, and he still did not consider the deputy's action was justified. Scott resumed.

'Even if Jeff knew it was Turkey, the boy was better off gettin' a couple of sharp nicks than runnin' into a hail of lead from Ben Yerby's guns. Don't you agree?'

Peake was still far from satisfied when Wagoner scrambled to his feet and led the visitor to the door. He laid a hand on the liveryman's shoulder and walked the boards with him to the other end of the street. The sheriff was tired, but curiosity was prompting him to go along and ask a question or two of the wounded youth before he turned in.

Turkey, who was not asleep, sounded startled when Peake called up to him that the sheriff wanted a word with him. The youth appeared at the top of the ladder and peered down at them.

'Turkey, is there anything you ought to be tellin' me right now?'

Wagoner sounded very formal, but he received no special information for his effort. He sighed, and tried again. 'Tell me, do you know the identity of the man who grooved you?'

Turkey shrugged and wriggled, and looked in every direction except at his questioner. Peake knew then that the sheriff had guessed right about the wounds. He was anxious for Wagoner to get back to his own quarters after that.

From the main door, the sheriff called: 'What did the fellow look like who gave you the information for Jeff Mays?'

'He was tall, not very old. Brown hair, ordinary trail clothes, an' a big brimmed hat. I couldn't see his features, wouldn't know him again, either!'

At that, Wagoner gave in. He emitted

a rather loud yawn, nodded to Peake, and stepped out into the street again. To his surprise, he saw a young stranger on a sorrel gelding reined in quite close to the door. Even a stranger at dusk could not raise any further interest in the weary sheriff that night.

Wagoner plodded back to his quarters, dragging the leg which suffered from his weak hip.

5

Turkey shared Baldy's surprise when the newcomer rode his sweating sorrel in through the big door and lightly sprang to the ground, knocking dust out of his clothing.

'You're kind of late, mister,' Peake remarked, looking him over.

'I've ridden most of the day comin' from the south, mister. I wouldn't want you to have to work late jest on my account. If you'd tell me where the oats is, I'll work on the gelding myself. That way, you can turn in.'

Peake managed a crooked smile. 'Sorry, mister, but this town's been a busy place today. Most of us have been out ridin'. I'll be glad to see to your cayuse. Why don't you mosey off down the street, get yourself fixed up with a bath an' somethin' to eat? The groomin' of one more hoss ain't goin' to break my back!'

The newcomer was a tall, sinewy young man in his middle twenties. His hair was thick, wiry and sandy-coloured. He wore a dun stetson, rolled in the Texas fashion, and a fairly new checked shirt. He looked as if he had worked around cows all his adult life. The outer ends of his blue eyes had acquired the Westerner's sun squint.

'Well, thank you, mister. I'll be glad to do jest as you say. Maybe I need the groomin' more than the hoss. The name's Red Richards, if you are interested. I shan't stray far. So long.'

Peake nodded and grinned. He left the stamping sorrel right where it was and went out to the grain bunker for more oats. In the short time he was away, Turkey scuttled down the ladder with his boots in his hand. He was given to frequent and sudden changes of mood, and the arrival of the stranger had partially caused this one.

Turkey's flesh wounds were paining him a little, but his vanity had been hurt a lot more. At that time, he did not know just how he felt towards Jeff Mays. Would an older man go along to the shack behind the courthouse and put a couple of bullets through the sleeping deputy's body? Was what had passed between them really an affair of honour, or had he — Turkey — really asked for the leaden warning by following up a man on a serious mission when he had no right to be in the vicinity?

He wondered if Jeff knew it had been him who had followed, or whether he thought it was someone else. Someone more vicious, more deadly even. For a minute or two the young man was so intent on his own thoughts that he did not notice that the redhead had left the sidewalk and stepped into the foyer of the Grand Hotel.

He walked on for a few yards and then stopped himself. Not knowing quite what to do with himself, he slumped down on a bench, and pushed his hat forward over his eyes. His chest heaved as he thought how he had been humiliated back there, to the north-west of town. He had lost face with the chief deputy. Things could never be quite the same between them.

But there was one thing which he knew, an item which he had not told the sheriff about, and that gave him a crumb of comfort. It was that flash of green. The earring with the green stone in it. He wondered if he could use his knowledge of the stone to his own advantage. It was hard to tell. He wouldn't really know the answer to that one until he met Jeff again, or heard what sort of a story he had put out.

At that moment, he was one of the very few people in town who did not know how Jeff had brought in the body of Yerby.

The redhead, another of those not in the know, stepped out of the hotel some ten minutes later. He paused for a moment and glanced up and down the street, listening and apparently smelling the atmosphere.

Two of the biggest saloons were doing a good trade. In one was a woman's voice, singing pleasantly to a piano which needed tuning. The other was noisier. The singers in that one were a whole crowd of men with untrained voices. The redhead chose the latter. He pushed back his hat, swung his legs along the sidewalk like a true son of the saddle, and crossed quickly towards the Blue Horizon.

Turkey waited for half a minute, and then followed him. He had eaten at Peake's place, but he was not averse to a glass or two of beer. Maybe he would get into conversation with the stranger, and find out something to his advantage. One of the youth's earliest lessons in life was about watching for opportunities.

Richards ordered whisky. He stuck out a big hand as the barman slid a bottle and glass along the bar to him. Soon the amber liquid had splashed into the glass and the first measure had been drunk. The redhead filled up again, and half emptied the second measure. He began to feel a little better. Some four or five men separated him from Turkey, who had called for beer and been ignored while older men were served.

Turkey studied himself in the mirror at the back of the bar. The day's business had left him a little pale, but his wounds did not show as Peake's handiwork was covered by the fringed coat. Only a faint stain of blood, partially washed out, gave any inkling of the kind of treatment that had been meted out to him earlier. He blushed as the barman served his beer with marked reluctance, and hurriedly raised his glass to his lips.

In the mirror, he studied the features of the redheaded man. He found himself imagining this fellow going against Jeff Mays as his champion. How would it be, he wondered, if the two men clashed head on with guns?

This stranger did not look like a gunfighter, but he looked capable enough. He had one Colt, well thonged down to his right thigh, and the gun belt was not gracing his waist just for show. The blue eyes flickered with sudden interest as though he knew that someone was taking a special interest in him. He glanced sideways along the bar, and Turkey chose that moment to examine the bottom of his beer glass for sediment.

He could be taller than Jeff, Turkey was thinking. Not much, maybe an inch, and possibly a few pounds heavier, too. The name, Red Richards, was not among the names which men remembered for their gun prowess.

The youth's conjecture had taken him just about as far as he could go when something happened to sharpen his interest in Richards. There was a sudden green flash across the redhead's knuckle. Others glanced along the bar at it, and so Turkey felt that he could look without betraying his special interest.

At first glance, the flashing green

stone looked as though it was embedded in a ring on the man's finger. But such was not the case. With his heart thumping with excitement, Turkey watched the adroit fingers so move that the stone came away from the finger. This was a coincidence, if ever there was one. The stone was embedded in silver; it was part of an earring such as he had had in his possession all those hours ago! The one which Jeff Mays had almost dropped! Could this be the same one? It would not be possible to know without asking directly, or getting information from Jeff in the morning.

It was an earring, all right. The redhead permitted it to slip away from his finger, and then to nestle in the palm of his hand. He seemed quietly gratified that so many strangers had taken an interest in it, even though none of them ventured a comment.

Turkey had a feeling that he would see the gem again. His intuition made him drain his glass and make for the batwings. In the gloom of the sidewalk, he waited, and within five minutes the man with the green stone came out again, rolling his fingers across his palm, as though he still had it in his hand.

Richards was studying the street again. He turned in the opposite direction, going on past a clean eating house from which was coming a savoury smell of food. Turkey began to follow him. Quick-witted as the lad was, he did not at first divine what the stranger was looking for.

The dim light of Samuel Ferraby's turned-down lamp brightened him at last. Ferraby was a short, thickset man in his early fifties. A skull cap made his frontal baldness seem complete. He could be seen as a shadowy outline behind another lamp directed over the bench where he did his clock and watch repairs.

Richards gave the shop window a good looking over. He stared shrewdly at the handful of clocks and watches and small jewellery on view, and promptly tried the door handle. The door opened under his hand and he stepped inside. Ferraby looked up, full of sudden interest, and then came forward to the serving counter, pulling his dressing gown more closely around him and taking his pince-nez off his nose.

'Good evening, sir. It isn't often I get customers as late as this, but you are welcome.'

'An' good evenin' to you, sir,' Richards replied, touching his hat and moving closer. 'I've got a bauble with me, an' I'd be glad if you'd examine it for me an' give me your opinion.'

Ferraby nodded, smiled and polished his watch glass. He took the earring from Richards with due consideration and carried it across to the brighter light, which he adjusted to its maximum brightness.

Richards had shown his earring on several occasions to jewellers in many different towns. He knew the approximate value of it, and it amused him to know how honest the jewellers were who appraised it.

'The emerald is a fine one, but the diamond, you understand, that is more valuable. Would you like me to estimate the worth of the whole thing?'

Richards nodded. The bright light and the stone drew the eyes of those in the shop, so that they did not notice Turkey peering in through the shop window. Before he could be seen by someone looking up suddenly, the youth ducked out of vision.

While Ferraby was still calculating, the redhead remarked: 'Have you by any chance seen one like it? The other half of the pair, perhaps?'

The jeweller shook his head. 'No, young man, I should have remembered if I had. It is quite a striking piece. But we were talking about its value. I would say today's price would be somewhere about forty or forty-five dollars. Yes, I think I could pay you forty-five for it, if you wanted to sell it. Or, on the other hand, I could make you an inferior replica for say, thirty dollars. Are you interested?'

'I'm grateful for what you have told me, sir, but I don't want to make any sort of a deal tonight. I shall be in town for a day or two and I may call on you again. I'll say goodnight to you now.'

'Good night, young man, and I hope you find comfortable lodgings! Adios.'

Richards left the establishment as quietly as he had arrived. The earring was back in his palm, and he was thinking that Samuel Ferraby was a fairly honest man. In a way, he was disappointed that no one in the saloon had shown any special attention to the jewel. Not enough to remark on it, anyway. Of course, if anyone had, it could have led to trouble.

With the jewel clutched in his hand, he sauntered on a little farther. Turkey, who was pretending to be hurrying the other way, collided with him at an intersection. Richards lost his hat and his balance, but when he straightened up, his chuckle suggested that he had not lost his sense of humour.

'Hey, mister, you sure are in a hurry. Are you hungry, or thirsty? Or is it both?'

Turkey took a really close look into Richards' face. In a few seconds he had satisfied himself that the redhead was indeed a total stranger, but Richards genially barred his path, waiting for an answer to his questions.

'Er, well, I'm sorry to barge you like that,' Turkey spluttered, 'but I can't rightly say I'm either thirsty or hungry. The fact is, I was on an urgent message, you see.'

Reluctantly, Richards stepped aside and gave him room to pass.

'Maybe I can persuade you to take a beer with me, in any case?'

Turkey shook his head and grinned. 'Not this time, amigo. Maybe in the mornin' when I have a little more time to spare.'

Richards allowed him to go off, and stood chuckling as the gap widened between them. He knew that Turkey had been in the saloon at the same time as himself, and he wondered whether in fact he was really engaged upon an errand at so late an hour.

Turkey, who knew Main Street and all the side turnings as well as anyone else in town, ducked down the side of a building and crossed the rear of three shops before cautiously re-emerging on the sidewalk and proceeding to the livery. He would have been surprised had he known that Richards was only twenty yards away when he opened the stable door.

The redhead left off his investigating at that point. He sought and found the food his body needed, and while he ate he listened to the gossip. The story of how Jeff Mays had brought in Ben Yerby made good listening while the food went down. Richards mulled over what he had learned, and returned to the saloon for some more beer.

As the hour was more advanced the drinkers were mellowed. They did not seem to mind when a stranger asked the details about the day's goings on. Finally, he sorted out two mature cattle dealers and casually asked them who the young fellow was who had been in there drinking beer earlier, the one with the fringed buckskin outfit.

'Fringed buckskin, huh? That'd be young Turkey, I fancy,' the older man opined.

'He was the man who took the message to the chief deputy, the note that told him where to meet Yerby,' the other added. 'Seems to me the lad had a spot of trouble on the way back, 'cause he was late reachin' town, an' he looked passin' pale to me.'

'Do you think he could end up in trouble for takin' the message about Yerby?' Red asked.

Neither of the dealers were sober enough for reasoned thought. One of them shrugged and yawned, while the other explained at great length that Yerby was too late to make trouble for the boy, as he was already on Slim Baron's slab.

Red pretended to find this comment highly amusing. His informers joined in. While they were still rocking with laughter, he left them and made his way to his room. He was tired, but he had plenty to think about.

6

As the first faint rays of daylight penetrated the building behind the court-house where the sheriff's personnel were privileged to sleep, Jeff Mays stirred and started to come awake. He had slept dreamlessly and without effort, but as soon as his eyes opened again problems connected with the previous day's happenings were back in his mind.

He could hear someone snoring in the next cubicle. It made him want to put off the explanations which were bound to be demanded. On a sudden impulse, he slipped from under his/ blanket, picked up his boots and grabbed his few items of toilet gear.

The door of the building had scarcely closed behind him when he pulled on his boots. Somewhere up Main Street a flea-ridden dog was howling, but otherwise the town was quiet. Walking quickly, he gradually left the populated end of the town behind and moved on to lower ground which led down to the banks of the turgid creek.

There, he traversed the bank until he came to a weeping willow. He fixed his mirror to a branch, stripped off his shirt and commenced to shave by means of soap and creek water.

Uppermost in his thoughts was Mirabelle and the earthy dugout where he had left her. He was seeing things in better perspective now. She would be uncomfortable, for sure. And perhaps she was not as safe as he had thought when he took her there. After all, Yerby had occupied his small ranch for some time; it was not beyond the bounds of possibility that some of the outlaw band knew the location of the cabin.

He was not at all sure how Mirabelle would fare in the event that the regular outlaws came looking for their habitual hideout and found Yerby missing. As the ranch was deserted, they might take over everything. On the other hand, the lack of personnel might drive them to search out where the residents had gone.

Sooner or later, they were bound to hear that Yerby, himself, was dead. But that would not explain what had happened to his wife, and to the boy and the old man who had worked there since Yerby took over.

Jeff sighed. He applied more soap and water to his left cheek and commenced scraping again. Then there was Turkey. Was he in town, or what? If he hadn't arrived, he might be on another of his foolhardy schemes: or he might have been the one who followed, and an unlucky ricochet could have done him a whole lot more damage than had been intended.

Almost certainly, Sheriff Wagoner would want to ride out in the same direction as the Yerby showdown in search of other outlaws. It would not do to dissuade the veteran lawman altogether from his purpose, because he could be right. There could be other outlaws hanging about in the direction of Bitter Spring Creek, and their presence would constitute a threat to Mirabelle.

At last he was satisfied with the smoothness of his chin. He rubbed his knuckles along it as he decided that he was ready for town and whatever awaited him. In fact, he was ready to ride, except for the emptiness of his stomach.

Ah Fong, the Chinese restaurant keeper, who operated at the west end of town, cooked him the meal he required, and forty minutes later he presented himself at the sheriff's office, bright-eyed and apparently keen.

Riders were already gathering for another day of posse work. Two men called out their congratulations to Jeff as he hovered by the door. Boris Groves noticeably drew farther away to avoid a meeting. Baldy Peake, the liveryman, was the one to go forward and actually involve Jeff in conversation.

'I don't know if you'd be interested, but Turkey's back. He came in late last night.'

Peake watched Jeff's expression intently. The interest was quick to show, and soon the frank blue eyes were returning the stare.

'I can't pretend I'm not interested, seein' as how Turkey was the one to bring a message to me yesterday. How is he? All in one piece?'

'Any special reason why he shouldn't be?' Peake asked guardedly.

Jeff shrugged. 'No, none that I can think of. But you don't seem to want to say your piece. Excuse me — '

The deputy was on the point of pushing open the door when Peake rather belatedly unloaded his information. 'He came in lookin' drained with two bullet burns. One was across his upper arm, an' the other on his hip. What do you think about that?'

'I'd say Turkey's been runnin' jest a little bit too close to serious trouble,' Jeff replied, without altering the tone of his voice. 'But I don't doubt you've done any patchin' that needed it, Baldy. Here's to another productive ride.'

Jeff grinned. He had just arrived indoors when Wagoner tightened his belt and prepared to emerge.

'Hm, it's about time, Jeff. Jest 'cause you brought in Ben Yerby don't mean you have to have the day off! I hope you slept well, 'cause I'm aimin' to make another big foray of the Yerby territory, an' *this* time you're goin' to be the guide! How does that suit you?'

Jeff stuck one boot on an upright chair and rotated a spur wheel. The metal circle was still spinning when he gave his reply.

'Well, it would suit me a whole lot more if there was a special rate of pay for guides! When do we start?'

'Right now, unless you can think of a really good reason for delayin' us. If you're hankering after that buckskin of yours, it's hitched round the back. Baldy brought it along with him, thought he was doin' you a favour.'

'He didn't sound all that friendly when he told me Turkey was back in town jest now!'

'Maybe you can understand that. Turkey is almost like an adopted son to Baldy.'

Sheriff and deputy faced each other. It was plain by Scott's tone that he thought Jeff responsible for Turkey's burns. Coming at a time when Jeff was not even sure about the matter himself, it either meant that the sheriff was very shrewd, or else a good guesser.

They put the issue from them and went outside to join the other riders.

Two Mile Rock came and went. Jeff took the riders in single file up the bear track, and eventually led them to the exact location where he had found Ben Yerby. In the last hour before noon, the deputy checked the watchful column and slid to the ground. A slight breeze had done much to alter the hoofprints on the track, and there was nothing in the dust which was likely to discredit the thin tale he intended to tell.

Scott and the other riders bunched around him as he pointed to the spot in the timber where Yerby had died.

'Actin' on information I came up this track. Some sixth sense made me do the last part very quietly. I came upon him in these trees doin' somethin' with the stallion. When he saw me, I expected him to use it as a shield, but he pushed it farther away.

'He saw the star on my shirt, an' I told him who I was. I named him, havin' seen his picture, and we decided that it would have to be a shoot-out on account of him not wantin' to surrender his weapons. So that's how it was. I don't remember a lot of details, so it ain't much use askin'.'

Jeff moved into the pines, propped his back against a tree bole and busied his fingers with the making of a cigarette. Scott stuck his pipe between his teeth and most of the other men dismounted.

Jeff kept his eyes down, not wanting to advertise the heightened colour in his face connected with his recent lies.

While his smoke was still burning, Jeff turned his attention to his Colt, dusting it and reloading it and all the time wondering what Mirabelle would be doing, and whether she would have company.

Scott Wagoner came towards him, clearing his throat. 'Jeff, if you were in charge of this party, an' you were real darned sure there was an outlaws' hideout close to this place, what orders would you give?'

Jeff's long straight nose looked thinner as he scowled. 'I wouldn't build up on findin' anythin' if I were you, Scott. After all, we've searched before an' got nowhere. I think maybe it might be a good thing if you split up the posse into small groups an' had them scour the ground in all directions.'

'I think I'll do that, Jeff, an' I don't figure we ought to be too down in the mouth. After all, this is the first search since you turned up Ben, an' if he was in the vicinity, he might have been near his base.'

Wagoner drew his men together. He split them into four groups. In charge of a group were Groves, Peake, Jeff and himself. Jeff took his men towards the east and he pretended not to be very interested in the direction taken by the others.

He was surprised to find that his group was the last to return to the shooting place around half past twelve. None of the leaders had anything worth while to add to what was already known about the area. Groves, who had gone west, spoke briefly about the valley in the direction of Bitter Spring Creek, but he had no enthusiasm for going farther in that direction.

Wagoner, who was irritated by the lack of developments, turned his gelding towards Jeff's mount and angled it towards him.

'Don't bother tellin' me you didn't expect anything. In this situation, where would you look next?'

'Down trail a piece. I have a feeling that might show up a well-hidden track or two.'

The deputy sounded anything but keen. He was wondering if the whole outfit could somehow be moved farther west, and that he could slip away from the others to contact Mirabelle without arousing unwanted curiosity. Wagoner lined up alongside of him, and, at a rather slow pace, they started back over the ground which they had already traversed.

The hollow where Mirabelle had hidden her mare on the occasion of Jeff's precipitate arrival was some fifty or more yards west of the track. Turkey, who was now using it, kept low until the sheriff and his posse had gone by on their way south. The youngster could tell by the riders' faces that they had not located any outlaws or found an outlaws' hideout.

The young man was keenly interested, otherwise he would not have come out from town with no chance of a reward for his labours on the day after he had acquired the two bullet grooves. He was still marvelling about Jeff having brought in Ben Yerby, a fascinating bit of information which Peake had given him the night before.

Turkey wondered if Jeff knew he was about to indulge in a gun clash with the notorious outlaw when he fired off the bullets to discourage his pursuer. His feelings towards the chief deputy at that moment were very mixed. He was not sure if he hated him, or whether he ought to admire him. Baldy had interested him further by telling him that Jeff wanted the reward money. Turkey would have liked a small cut of it for taking along the important message. He wondered if Jeff could be persuaded to part with some of the money, if he — Turkey — behaved really nicely towards him. It was hard to tell. Jeff hadn't ever been the sort of fellow anyone associated with *dinero* in large quantities.

As the distance between the hollow

and the last of the posse increased, Turkey became agitated. He fell to biting his nails and thinking over the possibilities of bringing the riders back again. On the previous day he had heard enough to know that Jeff's contact came from the west. He had not actually set eyes on the fellow, but it was plainly obvious, even to a youth crouching in terror, that the deputy's horse had halted not far from this hollow.

His curiosity about the previous day's events made him want to draw the posse farther west when he would not have gone that way alone. He thought about the consequences of such an act. His eye lit upon the lightweight Henry rifle in his hand, a weapon he seldom used.

He could bring the riders back by a gunshot. He did not have to show himself to influence them.

He was grinning as he pointed the gun skyward and fired off a single bullet. Having done this, he scampered across the hollow and clambered out on the west side, intending to get to horse and find himself a nice lookout spot from which to watch the posse go by.

The man on the other side of the pinto stood so still that at first Turkey failed to notice him. As the youth halted a few yards away, wondering whether he was in danger or not, the stranger stretched a little and glanced at him across the top of the saddle.

'Howdy, Turkey. Fancy us meetin' again after so short a time!'

Red Richards seemed to be completely at ease and fully in control of the situation. He chuckled and seemed to be highly amused by the way in which the youngster had lost the powers of speech.

'If you stand like that much longer, the posse will be up with you an' then you'll have to explain why you fired that bullet!'

Turkey's expression altered. He turned the muzzle of his gun towards the earth and approached purposefully, wondering if Richards intended to prevent him mounting his own pony.

'You must have been trackin' the posse to pop up unexpectedly like this,' Turkey accused.

'Not me, Turkey,' Richards argued firmly. 'All I did was follow you. You were the one showin' the special interest in the sheriff and his riders. You are still interested, otherwise you wouldn't have fired off your gun with the intention of drawin' them this way.

'Tell me, do you intend to run them into an ambush?'

'Eh, oh no. Nothin' like that. It's jest that I want them to do some searchin' a little farther west, that's all! What do you think I am, anyways?'

Red walked away from the pinto, turning his back on Turkey, who hastily mounted. When Richards had forked his own animal, the sorrel gelding, he turned it and waited for Turkey to come up with him.

'An interestin' question,' he remarked.

'I might think you're a thief, on account of you showed too much interest in the knick-knack I took along to Ferraby's shop last night. Now don't make out you're the sheriff's righthand man, will you, 'cause if you were, you'd have been out on the track an' stopped the riders instead of keepin' in cover an' firin' off your gun!'

They put another hundred yards or more between themselves and the hollow before glancing back again. By that time, hanging foliage was masking their movements from the bunched riders who were backtracking rather cautiously, on account of the gunshot.

'I'm not a thief, Red. An' there's a good reason why I haven't been out in the open talkin' to the sheriff. Right at this moment, his chief deputy, Jeff Mays, is sidin' him. You don't have any reason to know it, but Chief Deputy Mays almost shot me to death yesterday!'

Richards seemed surprised. He

looked his companion over and would have dismissed the charges, had not Turkey rapidly undone his tunic and showed the bandage on his left arm. He intimated the position of the other wound.

'So he gave you a couple of burns,' Red remarked after a short pause for thought. 'But you ain't tellin' me he mistook you for another of the Yerby outfit?'

'No, it wasn't like that at all. You see, I was followin' him. I took him a message earlier in the day, an' I wanted to know more. I didn't see that he ought to dismiss me the way he did, an' I thought it would be all right if I followed up behind. He didn't seem to think so. I tell you, I could have been dead!'

'You could, at that, but now that you know he brought in Yerby, don't you think he did you a favour in preventin' you followin' him any farther?'

Turkey pursed his lips, but did not whistle. That was another way of looking at the situation: a new one to him. He gave his attention afresh to Richards, who was looking for a suitable hiding place from which to observe Jeff Mays.

7

Jeff Mays entered the hollow and rode around it like a circus performer who specialised in tricks with horses. Sheriff Wagoner put his gelding into the saucer far more circumspectly, and the riders who were with them spilled out into a horseshoe shape round the rim of the landmark.

'There's no gainsayin' the fact that some hombre wanted us this way, Scott,' Jeff was saying, rather loudly. 'There's signs of a hasty withdrawal, an' I don't like that. It could be somebody wants to do the law a mischief. It might be a sort of reprisal for the killin' of Yerby.'

Having uttered these words, Jeff thought he had gone a bit far. It was unlikely that outlaws were so up to date with their plans, unless they were very well informed by spies or some such.

However, he did not withdraw his suggestion. He was still powerfully disturbed by the random shot which must have been fired to attract their attention.

Furthermore, it came from the hollow where Mirabelle had hidden her mare, and that consideration could mean something. He wanted to follow up the gunshot, and yet he knew that it could mean trouble.

'So, whatever it is, we investigate,' Wagoner instructed. 'At the first suggestion of snipin' we take cover. Otherwise, we ride westward an' see what we can find over the ridge.'

A good distance ahead, Red and Turkey conferred. They decided that the posse riders were coming on westward and that they were almost certain to ride on beyond the smooth hogsback ridge which blocked the view into the next valley.

Red would have ridden for the northern end of the ridge, that being the better way round, but Turkey knew

101

of the fault almost halfway along its length, a route which was considerably shorter. This local knowledge boosted the youth in the eyes of his companion, who began to study the way in which he handled the pinto and himself.

Turkey might be a little unpredictable, but he was certainly an interesting character. Likewise the tall fair deputy, seen through the spy-glass. A man who brought in an outlaw with the reputation of Yerby had to be.

'Why were you so interested in the earring?' Red demanded to know, as the fault absorbed them.

To Turkey, riding ahead, it seemed as if the redhead's eyes were boring into his back. He thought of two or three rather good lies, and then discarded them in favour of the truth.

'I don't see why I should have to tell you, but I will. You see, I saw an earring almost the same as yours only yesterday.'

Red almost lost his balance in excitement. He thought of all the places where he had enquired about the earring, and now, in wild country in Waterford County, in an atmosphere of outlaw hunting, here was his first real clue.

'Where did you see it?'

In his staccato, blustering manner, Turkey outlined the delivery of the envelope to Jeff when he was with the posse. He explained how curiosity had made him keep his eyes on the deputy long enough to see the green flash of the emerald and to see Jeff slip it into his pocket.

'Hey, are you sayin' this green emerald earring was sent along with a message to the chief deputy? The message about contactin' Yerby?'

'That's about the size of things, Red. Do you wonder I was curious when I saw you flashin' yours about in the Blue Horizon last night?'

'No, I'm not wonderin' about it any longer. In fact, I accept your explanation. Do you think Chief Deputy Mays will still have the earring in his pocket?'

'It's a nice question, but how would I know the answer? An' don't ask me who gave me the envelope for Jeff, either. They all do. All I can say is he was a young fellow, maybe about your own age, an' that he had brown hair an' ordinary horse-ridin' clothes. One of the reasons I'm out here now is because I thought we might run across him again.'

Red whistled. 'Such a meetin' might be very interestin'. Tell me, would you introduce me to the hombre, in the event he turned up unexpectedly?'

Turkey glanced back over his shoulder. 'I might,' he decided, after a pause. 'An' then again I might not.'

There were things these two men still did not know about each other, but during their ride together the beginnings of an understanding had begun to form between them.

Red Richards rode on in silence, blindly following Turkey, who had become his guide. His thoughts had turned inward, due to his riding partner's revelations of a few minutes earlier.

Red had acquired his earring from his father back in Phoenix, farther south in Arizona territory. It had been given to him at a time when his father, a medical doctor, had been assured that he — Red — intended to leave home.

The earring had once belonged to the doctor's first wife. She had been a full-blooded, well-bred Spaniard, a woman of restless disposition. The doctor's practice had kept him very busy, and, as a result, his wife had a lot of time on her hands. The day came when the Spanish wife packed a few things and quit her home for one south of the border in Mexico.

The doctor had been so far distracted that he wanted to go after her, but his son, his only son at the time, had persuaded him to stay and see if the wife came back. The doctor worked even harder to take his mind off his loss. A few years went by, and then they heard a report that she had been living in Sonora, and that she had recently died of a fever.

This news had been a blow and a relief to the doctor. Within twelve months he had married again. His second wife, Red's mother, was a redhead and a rancher's daughter. She had made the Doc very happy, and very little had happened to mar Red's childhood.

In fact, he was fully grown, and twenty-four years of age when tragedy struck a second time in the doctor's life. The sawbones was answering an emergency call. His wife had been on hand when he got the message and, consequently, she had gone along to drive the buckboard for him.

The speed needed to get to the emergency had been the cause of the accident. The wife had been standing up, and coaxing all possible speed out of the two matched horses when one of the wheels struck a stone and promptly turned the buckboard over.

The doctor had been shaken, but his

red-haired wife had fared worse. Her head had struck a huge boulder. She had been killed instantly. After pronouncing her dead, the doctor had stumbled along on foot to his patient and adequately coped with the tricky situation.

The loss of his wife, however, had hurt him. He was no longer the jovial doctor of old, although his patients swore he was just as efficient.

Red had been called home from the ranch on which he worked. The death of his mother had done things to him, too. He had matured, and become restless. The earring had been a last gift from father to son.

'Your older brother, half-brother of course, has the other earring, son. See if you can find him. He left home when I married your mother.'

Thus spoke the doctor as he parted from his younger son.

Red's half-brother was much older: in his late thirties by this time. He was heavier, too, and his hair was dark. He had been nicknamed Blackie in his youth. The doctor had not been able to give much guidance as to where to look for his older son. He had suggested a search farther north in the same territory.

There had been one other suggestion before they parted. Red was advised to keep his real name a secret until proper contact was made.

And now, it seemed, there was a sporting chance of meeting up with the owner of the other earring. Red was intrigued to know why the identical trinket had been passed to the peace officer. Perhaps it meant something special to him; in which case, it would pay to get to know Jeff Mays better.

In a very short space of time, the two mounted men were through the fault and resting up their horses in the valley beyond. There was more green vegetation about, but little sign of man or of habitations. Red paused in his grooming to ask a question.

'Hey, Turkey, am I right in thinkin'

we came this way because that elusive brown-haired fellow was seen around here?'

Turkey straightened up, out of breath. 'You're a shrewd fellow, Red. I can't say whether the brown-haired fellow actually came this far, but I know he came from the west side of the track down which the posse was ridin'. When they get into this valley, we might have a development of some sort, or we might not.'

Red built two smokes and handed one of them over to his partner.

'I don't figure you'll be in a hurry to meet Jeff Mays, but it will happen sooner or later. Why don't we casually ride to meet the posse when they get out this way, an' see how this Jeff hombre takes the meetin'?'

Red's presence gave Turkey confidence. By the time he had finished his smoke, he had made up his mind to contact the sheriff.

The meeting took place a half hour later, some two hundred yards across the valley floor. Turkey and Red came out of a timber stand and casually cantered across to converge with the larger group as if the meeting was entirely casual.

There were many curious glances from the men who made up the posse. Wagoner voiced the thoughts of many when he said: 'Well, Turkey, it's barely a day since you came ridin' up to us before, an' your message brought about Ben Yerby's downfall. Tell me, have you anythin' else to tell us, now that we meet miles from anywhere once again?'

'No, I don't reckon I have, Sheriff. I've been doin' a little scoutin' with my friend, here, but this far we don't seem to have made much progress.'

'There's folks back in town think it's my business to tell a young fellow like you not to go lookin' for trouble, Turkey. Especially does the advice seem timely in your case, seein' as how you got yourself shot at.'

At this point, Baldy Peake kneed his

mount forward and angrily asked for greater frankness about the previous day's shooting.

Jeff Mays was scarcely a yard away. He eyed Peake over very closely. 'Are you suggestin' *I* shot him, Baldy?'

'He thinks you shot Turkey offen your tail yesterday afore you went against Yerby,' Wagoner put in, in an effort to keep the peace. 'If you did that, I don't see any reason why you should withhold the facts.'

Jeff shrugged. 'Tell me, Turkey, did you follow me yesterday?'

The youngster swallowed hard. 'Sure, I was anxious to take another look at the fellow who gave me the message for you! I guess it must have been your bullets that hit me! They came off an outcrop of rock, an' they were fired like a man might fire them who was warnin' someone off!'

Jeff cleared his throat. 'I'm glad you ain't worse hurt, Turkey. You could have been, you know. An' right now, you're headin' right back into trouble. Surely bullet burns ought to be warnin' enough to stay in town. You're even tryin' to lead a posse by the nose. It was you who fired off that gun back there, wasn't it?'

Turkey was taken aback by this blunt accusation. A glance at Red's face, however, restored some of his confidence.

He blurted: 'Oh, that gunshot. Well, I was tinkerin' about with my gun an' it went off accidentally. An' the reason why Red an' me are west of the ridge is because I think the hombre with the brown hair, who gave me the message for you, is over this side some place.'

Speaking for the first time, Red remarked: 'We think the fellow who handed out the message might know a whole lot more about the outlaws, Sheriff. He seems to be the best hombre to question.'

For almost a minute there was silence. Jeff and several other men wanted Scott to ask the stranger what his business was in the area, but the question never came.

Instead, the sheriff said: 'You could be right, too. How about joinin' forces with us? We've got quite a lot of ground to cover in this valley.'

Turkey and Red exchanged glances. They both nodded. The entire party milled around for a few moments, and then broke off for a rest. When they were slaking their thirst, it seemed quite casual the way Red addressed his question to Jeff.

'By the way, Deputy, have you seen any more of that brown-haired fellow who sent you the message?'

Jeff's face went blank. 'Can't say I've met any man whose hair is noticeably brown, mister. Other than some of the riders in the posse, perhaps, an' they don't seem to have time to walk around with their hats off. Besides, Turkey would be the one to identify him, if he showed up, not me.'

Red accepted the explanation. He shrugged, raised his brows in Turkey's direction, and strolled off. The sheriff and several others seemed mildly disappointed by Jeff's indeterminate reply.

8

The valley stretching north and south beyond the hogs-back ridge was well defined. Jeff knew that inevitably someone would stumble upon the ranch which had been Mirabelle's home in this county. How long it would take to find he did not know. Having been there already, he did not want anyone to guess that he had seen it.

He offered little in the way of advice when the enlarged riding party was split up again into four groups. As a result, the sheriff offered him control of the second group, a party which would deal with one flank or the other in the north-east search. Without wanting to seem too interested, he chose the western flank. That suited him best because the dugout was over in that direction. Obviously, he would not have the chance to slip out of the valley alone, and the next best thing was to see that posse riders did not become too venturesome in Mirabelle's direction.

Boris Groves, the jailer, had charge of the group which scoured land farther south. Wagoner himself took the east flank of the valley, while Peake, Turkey and Red Richards led the fourth bunch directly towards the north.

Jeff kept his anxieties from the five riders with him.

It was obvious that Baldy Peake's party would make the find, but would the ranch be occupied when they arrived there? In the event that outlaws had finally gone to earth there, two or three rifles could easily empty half a dozen saddles, if the approaching searchers were not careful.

Jeff felt bad enough over Turkey's superficial wounds. He did not want other wounded riders on his conscience. From time to time his men poked about under scrub and stunted trees on the western rim of the valley and shot brief questions at him. They found him withdrawn and hard to communicate with. Sometimes they mumbled about him, but their confidence in him remained unshaken. A deputy who could bring in Ben Yerby feet first would take a long time to lose his prestige.

In the fleeting intervals when he could put his problems aside he wondered what these hard-working Westerners would think of him if they knew all the facts about what had happened the previous day.

Another thing puzzled him. Was Turkey leading this newcomer into the investigation, or had the redhead got some special reason for tacking himself on to the sheriff's posse? Any stranger who happened along now was a potential enemy. He could possibly be an outlaw who had tacked himself on to the forces of law and order so as to give himself a cover and to be well informed as to what the sheriff was doing out of town.

And yet the redhead did not look like a man who earned his living by the gun.

Jeff glanced around. None of the other groups was in sight. The only visible sign was a small patch of dust way over to the eastern extremity. To the south, Groves was making a meticulous search, and farther north the Peake group was probably travelling fastest of all.

The deputy yawned. He tired of his mundane task. 'Hey, fellows, why don't you come down the slope another fifty yards or so? You'll find the goin' easier. Me, I'll move up a little higher an' see if there's any sign among these copses!'

The nearest men nodded. Their interest was flagging. It was the middle of the afternoon. Had they been travelling alone they would have been dozing in the saddle. Their progress was a little quicker. Jeff began to drop slowly behind because of the weaving he had to do around the tree clumps.

About thirty minutes later, a tree branch swept off his hat. He stiffened suddenly and realised that he must have dozed. Seeing him dismount, the other riders in his bunch backtracked, thinking he was pausing for a rest.

Only the party to the north was making positive progress.

With no badge wearers to dissuade him, Turkey had ridden fast so that he was almost a hundred yards ahead when he entered the timber break which hid the Yerby holdings from the south. He rode through the trees with his body tensely crouched. As the trees thinned out, he saw the buildings at a slightly lower level, in front of him.

Genuine surprise prevented him from yelling his head off straight away. Instead, he pulled out a spy-glass and trained it on the buildings, carefully looking for signs of life. All he could see was a mongrel dog, which looked as if it did not really belong in the yard, and a couple of prowling chickens.

The eight or ten mustangs were in a wired enclosure, wide of the buildings on a grassed slope. Horses, but no riders.

Behind him, Turkey could hear the steady approach of his friends. His courage came back to him. He had been the one to find the ranch, probably the outlaw hideout, so why shouldn't he go ahead and be the first one to enter it?

He felt over the bandages which protected his real wounds, and even then he was not put off. He dug his heels and spurs into the pinto's flanks and felt the beast shoot forward under him. A minute later, they were out in the open and starting over the down-grade towards the distant buildings.

He might have lost face the previous day, but he would make up for it today!

'Ho, there! I found the place! Me, Turkey! Ain't I the scout of all scouts?'

He commenced yipping at the top of his voice. His cayuse increased its speed without knowing quite why. No ordinary voice would have checked the youth's forward progress, but the three rifle bullets, fired in swift succession, did.

Turkey hunched his shoulders and hauled back on the reins. His neck muscles were stiff as he peered back up the slope. There was Baldy with the smoking rifle, sided by Red and the others. He relaxed with an effort. Those three bullets had gone less than a yard over his head, and for a few seconds he had believed outlaws to be at his back, rather than friends.

Red shouted: 'Hold on right there, Turkey!'

He employed a tone of voice which did not permit of any argument. Turkey did better than just hold on, he turned his pinto around and walked him slowly back to his friends. Peake was coldly angry, and Red apparently approved of his anger, although the rest of the dusty riders were more interested in the buildings than in Turkey's behaviour.

'Don't you know you could have been ridin' straight into a hail of lead, for the second time in two days?' Red admonished him.

'But I had me a good look-see through the glass, Baldy!' the youngster protested to the older man.

'Outlaws are too cautious to show themselves to any young hombre who's still wet behind the ears!' Peake pointed out. 'All right, so you found the place. But when we go forward, we go together. Sheriff Wagoner wouldn't like it if he found his posse men dead on the ground when he gets here!'

A minute went by, during which every available glass was turned on the ranch set-up. At last, Peake gave the order to go forward. The horsemen cantered down the slope, watchful all the time, the blood pounding through their veins.

In the last fifty yards, Turkey's patience gave out; he urged the pinto ahead as though getting there first was a matter of life and death. He was some ten to fifteen yards ahead of Red Richards when he leapt the gate of the paddock and pulled up in front of the house with one of his customary spectacular stops.

Peake and the rest of the riders cautiously surrounded the other buildings with rifles and revolvers at the ready. No one emerged, however, to deny their right to take over.

Turkey soon forgot his fears. He prowled the house, studying the bedrooms, the dining room and the kitchen, and deciding that Yerby, if this had been his place, knew how to live decently. The furniture was neatly cushioned. The curtains had been tastefully chosen.

Half way through his second survey, Turkey encountered Red in the kitchen. He was studying the dead embers in the bottom of the stove.

'Plenty of bedding, clothing about. All kinds of house equipment, everything,' Turkey remarked.

Red nodded. 'All it lacks is people. I'd say more than one man ran out on this place in the past few days. It's lacking in details, photographs, the sort of things which mark it as the property of a particular group of people.'

Red went very thoughtful. As others entered the house after prowling the other buildings, he pulled out his Bull Durham sack and tossed it to Turkey to do the cigarette making.

Letters and pictures might be scarce, but there was one indication which could not be ignored, and that was significant. Burned into the gate posts, and in other places was a big letter 'D' set in a round circle. A branding letter which might or might not be on the hide of those half-wild ponies out in the enclosure.

Red gave that Circle D a great deal of thought.

Within the hour the whole of the Waterford riding party had occupied the Yerby ranch. Turkey had enough admiring glances to keep his spirits high. He even waylaid Jeff Mays as he hitched up his horse at the rail in front of the house.

'Say, Jeff, could I talk to you a minute?'

'All right, what is it, Turkey?'

'Seein' as how I brought the important message to you yesterday, how about givin' me a part of the reward money for bringin' in Yerby?'

Jeff straightened up beside the tired buckskin. 'Well, that's straight talkin',' he acknowledged. 'An' here's a straight answer. You had nothin' to do with bringin' in Yerby. That bein' so you don't get a part of the reward. I have a special use for it.'

Red Richards, who was close, started to chuckle in a rather grim fashion. 'Pardner, I'd say the deputy was tellin' you to get an outlaw of your own. Maybe you'll be lucky before this trip is over.'

Jeff did not wait to reply. He ducked under the gallery rail and made his way into the house to carry out an inspection every bit as thorough as the earlier ones. He marvelled that Mirabelle had cleared out so many things of

125

a personal nature. But then, she had always been a clear-headed young woman.

Gradually, the party congregated in and around the front gallery.

Groves was the one who remarked: 'Seems like Yerby was married, huh? But no wife here right now . . . '

Every member of the group had clearly envisaged a swift evacuation.

After a useful meal, eaten with guards posted, Scott Wagoner held a big parlay of his most responsible men. Their opinion was that the ranch might still be used by renegades on the run from Dwarf Canyon or other places.

'Tonight, we occupy the buildings an' keep a strict watch,' the sheriff ordered. 'Also, I want a party to do some more ridin' over towards the east of here. They might jest happen upon riders comin' in by moonlight. Ridin' or jest watchin' will be tirin' work. I want this work done thoroughly. Now, who's goin' to suggest how we split the forces?'

After further discussion, the men were divided up three ways. To Jeff fell the distinction of guarding the house itself. He had with him Turkey and Red Richards and four others. Wagoner himself, and another seven men were thinly scattered around the bunkhouse, the cook shack, the stable and the barn.

To Boris Groves, the other deputy, fell the distinction of taking charge of the night riders. He had in support Baldy Peake and six more riders.

The men in the buildings went to their places a half hour after sundown. The sound of Groves' riders clearing ranch range lulled them into a sense of security. Jeff found himself nodding in the big dining room by the window.

He wandered through to the kitchen and informed two men watching on that side that he was going out on the gallery for a while. Another man asked that the watch-keeping might be split. Jeff was agreeable. He sent four men off to sleep, with orders to call the watchers in two hours.

Less than an hour had gone by when an arm reached out through the open dining-room window with a revolver in it. The butt of the weapon descended upon the side of Jeff's head, robbing him of his senses. A body went out through the window and made a thorough search of his pockets.

The searcher, who had been looking for the earring with the green stone in it, retired disappointed.

9

The time was within fifteen minutes of midnight.

A pale, scudding moon made little impression upon the darkened sky some three days after the latest shootings in and around the stores of Dwarf Canyon. At that hour of the night, not many men were abroad.

The two men on horseback three miles north-east of Ben Yerby's hideout ranch seemed to have the world to themselves. For the past two days they had rested in daylight and moved at night. It was a mode of travel which they had often used. The claybank and the roan gelding which carried them slowly and carefully westward in the direction of Bitter Spring Creek had often shared such jaunts, and they scarcely ever put a foot wrong.

For an hour their keen eyes had been

watching the trees and general foliage etched against the dark sky. Now, they were tired and ready for any kind of a diversion.

Jinx Farrimond, a man with a black drooping moustache which paralleled his mouth, suddenly gave out with a skittering laugh. His Roman nose was prominent under a stained dun stetson, the brim of which was broken at the front. He had small, hard eyes which almost closed when he grinned.

His partner, Lon Birk, was startled by the sudden outburst. He admonished Farrimond for it, and pointed out that a man's nerves were not at their best at this hour of the night when travel was necessary.

Almost as an afterthought, Birk asked: 'Anyways, what in tarnation is there for a man to laugh at in our situation?'

Birk was thirty-five years old and six feet tall although he did not look to be that height on horseback on account of his stooped shoulders. He had a full jowl and a thick underlip which appeared sizes too big for his otherwise lean body. His head, under the undented hat, was bald. In fact the hair on his brows and eyelids was sparse, and he seldom looked in need of a shave.

Farrimond laughed again before answering.

'I was thinkin' about Yerby's wife. That no-good ranch-minder sure does know how to pick them, Lon. An' one of these days some of the boys are goin' to be lucky enough to meet her when her old man's in town, or somethin'!'

Birk broke a matchstick and stuck it in between two teeth, gouging out a piece of bacon which had lodged there. 'So that's why you were soundin' off. Well, I'll allow she's a very fine-lookin' woman, but you ought not to go entertainin' any special thoughts about her. Any sort of impolite talk about her always brings out the worst in Yerby, who might still kill for her.

'Besides, there's Rock. Ain't you ever

seen the way Rock's blue eyes twinkle when he first sets eyes on her? Why, she has such an effect on him it almost cures his squint!'

Farrimond had gone quiet. 'I can't say I recollect seein' Rock oglin' her, Lon. Still, if you've noticed it, perhaps he does fancy her. Anyways, he ain't likely to be here ahead of us this trip.'

Birk yawned. 'There's truth in that last statement, all right. If they all did as Rock said after partin' this side of Dwarf Canyon, no one is likely to make the ranch for a day or two after we get there. I don't figure our early arrival will do us much good, though, except that we can rest properly!'

'Say, how much longer do we have to plod along in this direction, Lon?' Farrimond queried, as he knuckled his eyes.

'We could hit the creek in another hour, amigo. It's a long way round, but it sure is the safest at this time of night. Soon as we make the water, we'll freshen up, then it'll be a straight short ride south!'

Farrimond was about to answer when he heard a strange sound.

'This sure is borin',' Birk went on, 'it has me wishin' someone would chase us again. At least the excitement would be back again, that'd be somethin'!'

'Maybe it is back,' Jinx murmured. 'Somethin' happenin' over that way.'

According to pre-arranged practice in these circumstances, both men reined in their mounts, slid to the ground and held the animals by the muzzles. Their ears were straining now for a recurrence of what Farrimond heard earlier.

Again there was a creak of saddle harness, and a bit tinkled. The outlaws stiffened. Very carefully, Farrimond gave a special owl call. They heard voices, signifying that it had been heard by other men, but the special response was not forthcoming.

'Seems like there's maybe six of them, comin' right across us, if we ain't careful,' Birk murmured.

'I figure we blast them an' then carry on, same as before,' Farrimond suggested.

Birk nodded. Out came their shoulder weapons. Standing side by side with a boot firmly trapping their reins to the ground, they lined up on the searching party and awaited the most telling moment.

Flame blossomed briefly from Farrimond's weapon a second before Birk was ready. Then they were levering and firing together. For something like two and a half minutes they fired bullets at the riding group. Cries of two kinds came back to them. Some were from hurt men, and others merely indicated the posse was startled.

By the time two rifles were firing back at them from cover close to the ground, the outlaws had had enough. They sheathed their weapons, swung up into leather and headed due west, as before. They had much to think about now, and nothing to gain by a discussion.

Six men continued to fire after them, although their position could only be guessed at. Leading the posse now was a dark-skinned swarthy man named Rex Burgh. Usually, Burgh was quiet and withdrawn from his fellows on account of a bronze tint to his skin which betokened Indian blood. He was very muscular and capable, however, having worked as a blacksmith and then a saddler.

Burgh panned his rifle with real skill, guessing at the riders' direction. Shortly before he gave up using ammunition, he went close enough to singe Farrimond's bandanna with a good shot.

Boris Groves had been nicked rather badly at waist level and also on his shoulder. As the firing died out, he began to fight down the growing pain and bemoan his lot.

'Hey, Baldy, what were you thinkin' about to let us ride straight into an ambush? I thought you claimed to have the sharpest senses in the outfit? If I'd have known this would happen you'd have been bringin' up the rear. I never did care much for liverymen, in any case.'

Burgh cleared his throat. 'If I were you, Groves, I'd stop soundin' off. You see, you're wastin' your time. Peake is dead. There'll be a new liveryman in his place one of these days.'

Groves gasped. He murmured his regrets for what he had said and asked for help with his wounds. Burgh, when asked, confirmed that the gunmen had ridden out of earshot and that it would be safe to strike a match and do a little patching up.

There was a discussion about the direction in which the gunmen were heading. Obviously, they would turn north or south at the creek. It was decided that Groves' party could not do anything to further the action. If the outlaws turned south, the garrison of the ranch would get them. If they went north, they would remain free to rob another day. Slowly, the mauled party set itself to rights and began to retrace its steps.

★ ★ ★

A full half hour passed before Jeff Mays recovered from the blow on the head. He found his senses still reeling when he recovered consciousness on the front gallery of the ranch house, and for a time he had no clear idea as to what had happened. He laid his cheek against the boards of the floor and solemnly blinked his eyes, waiting for the clear return of memory.

The faint sound of the curtain flapping inside the window gave him a clue. He glanced round at it and partially remembered. He was with the posse, and they were hunkered down in Ben Yerby's ranch, waiting and hoping for the approach of other outlaws.

But what had happened to his head? He had a strange throbbing in it which was unaccountable. He could not remember having banged it on anything, or of anyone approaching him. Altogether he was mystified, and the contents of his stomach were not at all settled within him.

He kept as still as possible. Ten minutes later a single figure, a man with a slight limp, made a cautious tour of the buildings. By the paddock gate, Wagoner paused.

'That you, Jeff, on the gallery? Jeff?'

The deputy, whose head was spinning again, made a sound which was really a groan.

'I figure that flurry of noise was shootin' up to the north. Probably Groves an' his squad in a little action. We go on exactly as before. If our boys come back they give the signal. Anybody else comin' in close gets a brief warning an' then a blastin'. That all right by you, Jeff?'

With a big effort, the deputy raised his head. Suddenly he lost control again. His head flopped with rather a bump, his hat came off and the sheriff grumbled at him for not acknowledging properly. Shrugging his shoulders, Wagoner trudged on, anxious to get back to the comparative comfort of his vigil spot in the bunkhouse.

At the end of two hours, the ranch had still witnessed no alarms. A man named Bummer Peters came along and shook Jeff.

'Time's up, Deputy. I'll take over right here, if that's all right to you?'

Peters was a short, energetic little man, quiet and swift in his movements. He shared his ordinary working time between the hotel, where he was the general handyman, and the Blue Horizon saloon, in which he worked as part-time barman. He seemed surprised to find Jeff in a comatose state. Here, he had imagined, was one man guaranteed not to sleep at his post.

'Can you see anythin' wrong with my head, Bummer?'

Bummer cautiously touched Jeff's head and at once noticed the big swelling over his right temple. 'What did you do, bust your head on the window, or somethin'? No wonder you're lookin' drowsy, Jeff. I'll help you indoors, if you like!'

'Don't bother, amigo. My head ain't all that clear yet. If I can get down to the pump and use some of that water maybe I'll feel better, eh?'

Peters grinned, shrugged and stepped aside. Jeff picked up his Winchester and his hat, and managed to negotiate the three steps. He disappeared round the end of the gallery, still walking rather unsteadily in the direction of the pump. Bummer declined to watch his further progress. Instead, he went back to Jeff's observation post and made himself comfortable on an old mat.

Farrimond and Birk dismounted and walked the last half-mile of the protracted night journey. The creek had veered away from them to westward. They knew the ranch was close, but just how close they were not certain.

'Three days since the raid, an' that posse still active, Jinx. In the middle of

140

the night, too. They must have had some sort of success to keep them keen for so long. What do you think?'

Farrimond was not anxious to air his inner forebodings. He knew Birk's reasoning was sound, but where did it lead them?

'I don't see how they could have had a tip-off as to where we are, because we ain't really met anybody since we left the rest of the boys. So that brings us round to your theory. They've done themselves a bit of good. But *what* good?

'Is it somethin' to do with the other boys, or has somethin' happened at the Yerby place? I hate to think it, but I think they might have rumbled old Ben.'

Now that it appeared as if the hideout might have been discovered, Ben Yerby was receiving mention in a rather more friendly fashion.

'If your reasonin' is right, we're walkin' straight into trouble,' Birk opined. 'Except that we are wide awake.

Six or seven riders ain't much of a number for a sheriff's posse. It wouldn't surprise me if there were three or four times that number prowlin' around the canyon country, so help me, it wouldn't.'

'If they are, what do we do?' Jinx murmured. 'I mean, where do we go?'

Lon Birk sighed. 'Well, we pull out again with as little fuss as possible. Then, seein' others may be in danger, we do our best to get farther east again. We make a big detour around Waterford an' slowly approach Studley. Ye know we have to go to Studley in the near future?'

'Oh, sure, I ain't forgettin' Studley an' the next job, but bein' on the run all that extra time, it certainly makes a change for the worse, don't it? I mean, we could be spotted any time. We can't always expect to be as lucky as we were back there.'

'Things don't look too good, Jinx, but they could be worse. Anyways, they'll seem better in the mornin'.'

Birk managed a grim chuckle, but Farrimond could not match him for that. He was thinking that it was the hours before morning which were critical, and that they might not be together and breathing when the sun came up.

Birk stuck out a hand, restraining his partner.

'We can't take the hosses any closer. They'd give us away.'

Farrimond nodded rather gloomily. He helped to pin them out and then signified that he was ready to go on. Knowing the location of the semi-wild ponies, they gave the enclosure a wide berth. One thing became clear as soon as they overlooked the home buildings. The regular homing lamp was not burning.

Jinx became edgy then. 'Let's back out, amigo. We've seen enough. There could be another rovin' patrol at the back of us. Me, I'm not sure I wouldn't sooner ride right out of this county an' look for opportunities somewhere else.'

Birk patted his arm. 'I've often felt that way. It may not pay off. This sort of life is full of tight situations. Besides, we'd have to forfeit our share of the last job, an' that's worth pickin' up.'

Jinx quietened, but Birk was not ready to leave until he had assured himself that the ranch was unhealthy. He received his confirmation when he heard a couple of fretting horses in the stable. They were fretting because the stable was new to them.

Shoulder to shoulder, the partners started the walk back. The big detour to Studley was going to need a whole lot of patience, and luck, if they were to make it unnoticed.

10

Dawn was a half hour away when Turkey blundered through the ranch house and made a rather noisy contact with Bummer Peters on the front gallery. Bummer was startled.

He murmured: 'Is — is that you, Jeff? I've been expectin' you for a half hour! Time sure does drag at this hour of the night.'

Peters started to scramble stiffly to his feet.

'Here, this ain't Jeff Mays, amigo, it's Turkey. Are you tellin' me Jeff ain't around? I was wantin' to ask him about that pony snickering over there. My pardner reckons it's in the enclosure, but I don't think so.'

'Aw, shucks, I couldn't say, Turkey. At this angle, an' in this light it sure is difficult to know where the boundaries of that hoss enclosure are.'

145

Turkey removed his hat and scratched his head. 'If Jeff ain't here, then where is he? Surely you've done your time, as you were sayin'. He should be takin' his second spell. Shouldn't he?'

'You know darned well he should be, an' how can I say where he is? Ain't I been watchin' the shadows till my eyes are jest about crossed? I ain't seen him since he went round the corner of the buildin' to the pump.'

'Yer, yer, Bummer. I didn't mean to rile you. You must be good an' tired. How would it be if I slipped out there an' had a look-see where Jeff is? He could have gone over to the sheriff to have a talk about somethin'.'

Peters looked doubtful. He shrugged his shoulders, sank to his knees, and reluctantly agreed. 'All right, only don't be away long. I can't guarantee to keep on the alert much longer.'

Turkey patted Bummer on the shoulder in a fatherly fashion. He eased himself through the gallery rail and moved silently towards the end of it in a pair of mocassins which he had found in the house.

He had drawn water the previous evening and the location of the pump was known to him. He paused by a bench against the end wall of the house and then set off confidently, though slowly, in the direction of the pump.

Although he was not moving quickly, he had stumbled over the body before he was aware that it lay on the ground. His feet went from under him and he landed heavily, jarring his hip wound and losing his stetson. Two common oaths had cleared his lips before he remembered to maintain silence.

'Who is that?' the prone man asked.

Turkey sucked in breath. 'Jeff, is that you? This is me, Turkey. I didn't see you lyin' there an' I stumbled over you. You ain't makin' out I did it on purpose, are you?'

'Doggone it, how long have I been lyin' here? Ain't that the pump over there? I guess I never made it. Turkey, I need some water. Did Bummer tell you about the lump on my head?'

'Why no, he never said anythin' like that, Jeff. If you could get as far as the pump I could work the handle an' slosh some water over you. Maybe you'd feel better after that.'

'No, not that,' Jeff argued. 'It would be too noisy. Most of the watchers must have heard you fall over me already. Go an' get the bucket that stands under it. I figure it'll be full, an' that'll be enough for my purpose.'

Turkey went off then and he succeeded in getting to the pump and bringing back the full bucket without any further stumbling. Jeff pulled off his hat and bandanna and signalled for the water to be poured over him. More puzzled eyes glanced towards the pump area from the other buildings, hearing the faint sound of water.

Jeff let the water drip off him. He coughed quietly while Turkey stood above him, holding on to the empty bucket.

'Are — are you feelin' any better, Jeff? You want I should help you back to the house?'

Jeff's stomach was still a little unsettled but his head was clearing for the first time since the blow on his head. He repeated in his thoughts what Turkey had just said, and told himself who was talking.

'Er, no, I don't want you all that close, Turkey,' he remarked tersely. 'Jest lead the way back to the house an' I'll follow you. I ain't likely to pass out again, so don't bother your head any more.'

With an effort the deputy moved to his knees and rose unsteadily. He swayed for a moment, waved away his helper and started back towards the building. An upright at the end of the gallery comforted him.

Bummer's voice whispered: 'Are you all right now, Jeff?'

He sounded curious, but not curious enough to listen to a detailed explanation before he had slept. Jeff murmured: 'Yer, away you go, Bummer. You must be dead tired. I'll be along there in a minute. I — I have to talk with Turkey on a rather important matter.'

Bummer murmured his thanks and faded through the door into the house. Turkey stood against the wall of the building, cuddling his rifle and biting a thumb nail. Jeff sank into a wicker chair and cursed as it creaked.

'Turkey, I appreciate you gettin' that water back there, but there's other things we need to talk about. About this lump on my head, for instance. An' how it came to be there.'

Turkey peered down into Jeff's face. He noted that the deputy did not look so confused. His expression was a stern one, almost as if he was accusing Turkey of having put the lump on his skull.

'Are you suggestin' somebody put that bump on your head on purpose? Somebody who wanted you unconscious?'

Turkey's voice faded. Jeff nodded. Once was enough to remind him that his head was in a tender state. 'That's about the size of things. I figure a hand came through that window an' fixed me when I was lyin' prone on the boards out here. Now, who could have wanted me unconscious? Puttin' me out of action wouldn't have improved the outlaws' position so it must have been somebody who bore me a grudge. Someone in the house, see?'

Turkey thumped his chest. 'You mean me, don't you? Me, Turkey!'

From the bunkhouse there came the sound of a throat being cleared. Voices were carrying, but the two arguing men were past caring about that, for the time being.

'You have good reason to dislike me. On account of your bullet burns, an' bein' refused a share in the reward money for Ben Yerby. Was it you, Turkey? If not, who else could it have been?'

The youngster bit off an angry retort

151

as a possible name suggested itself to him. After a pause, he made his protest. His voice went up a tone or two, due to his anger. Jeff had risen to his feet and was looking quite belligerent. His rifle was discarded and he was reaching out for Turkey's tunic.

'I tell you I didn't do it! What could I have gained, except workin' off a bit of spite on you, will you tell me that?'

'Wasn't that why you did it? For spite?'

Jeff had him by the shoulders and was prepared to try and shake a confession out of him when Sheriff Wagoner's angry whisper halted the altercation.

'You two men on the gallery! Go indoors an' keep quiet. I'm comin' over there myself, an' I wouldn't be either of you if you give warnin' of this ambush after all these hours of waitin'!'

Jeff was too pent up to speak. He pushed Turkey before him, indoors, and at once became aware of hostile eyes regarding him through the darkness.

Turkey broke away from him, and went into one of the bedrooms.

Three minutes later, Scott Wagoner came in through the back door. He stalked through the house and found his chief deputy leaning against the frame of the front door, solemnly dabbing drops of water off himself with a damp bandanna. Scott took Jeff by the arm and steered him out on to the gallery.

The sheriff was so rattled he would not trust himself to do a lot of talking. Instead, he asked Jeff for an explanation. He had to lean close to catch all the details. They were few and mystifying.

When he had finished, Scott said: 'So you've been out cold, unconscious, for maybe two and a half hours?'

'That's so, an' was on the point of shakin' a confession out of Turkey when the noise attracted you.'

'You think it must have been Turkey?' Scott queried, after inspecting the contusion.

'Who else could it have been?'

Scott ignored the question. Instead he surveyed the grey landscape which had taken up so much of his attention throughout the night. He could not remember when his eyes had been so tired.

He opined. 'No outlaws are likely to hit this place tonight. In fact night is almost over. You can see dawn threatenin' over there. I can't understand it. Maybe Groves' party can throw some light on what's been goin' on when they get here. I'm disappointed.'

The sheriff became restless. He prowled through the house, and asked one of the men watching at the back to take over at the front. This done, the two badge-wearers settled down on either side of the stove in the kitchen. Scott fed kindling wood into it and lit it, setting the coffee pot on top.

'Jeff, some of your behaviour lately has baffled me. This latest thing, for instance. Obviously somebody hit you, an' Turkey would be the first fellow you'd think of, but it didn't have to be him, did it? I think you've been keepin' certain details back from me, ever since you got the message regardin' Yerby. I ain't sayin' you haven't got a right to keep some of the details back, but are you sure there isn't anythin' of a helpful nature you've held from me this far?'

The fair man thought back over the whole affair. He had not liked keeping back facts from his old riding partner. It had seemed the only thing to do. This time, his thoughts focused upon Yerby's last minutes.

Suddenly, he gripped Scott's arm. 'Yes, there is somethin' I should have told you, Scott. Can't think why I didn't mention it before. Maybe that blow on the head did a bit of good, after all! As he was dyin' I tried to get him to help the law. All he was able to say, Yerby, I mean, was to keep a watch on Studley. He did a funny thing with his finger, drawin' it across his throat like — like a Mex might threaten to cut it, an' then he gave up the ghost! I'm sure he was on the level, though.'

The new information had brightened the sheriff. 'Studley, eh? Seems like the gang was plannin' on raidin' Studley next, then. I wonder where they'd be likely to strike? Studley is quite a thriving place, bein' a railroad town.'

In spite of Scott's excitement, Jeff's thoughts were centring on Mirabelle now. Already he was toying with the badge which should have been pinned to his shirt.

'Scott, all I've told you is true, except for a few minor details. There are good solid reasons for me changin' my attitude in the past few days, reasons you'd probably approve of if you knew about them. I've hung on with the posse till you found this place. Now, I want out. I have things I still want to do, an' it's better I'm not wearin' a badge when I do them. I can't expect you to fully understand, or to approve my actions, but I do have to go, an' now seems as good a time as any.'

Jeff tossed the badge on the table

where it wobbled and then became still.

'Where in tarnation am I goin' to find another chief deputy at a time like this?' Scott protested.

'Take it easy, amigo,' Jeff replied. 'There has to be a change over of personnel now and again. Why not give Groves a try? He has certain drawbacks, but he tries hard. After all, he took the roughest job this time, ridin' at night! Maybe he deserves a boost!'

'You didn't talk that way when you punched him all round the sidewalk an' then dumped him in the trough,' the sheriff argued drily. 'Still, if he's the only one, seemingly he'll have to be promoted. Do I take it that if I accept your badge now you won't be interested in my type of work any more?'

Jeff shrugged. 'I think that would be assumin' too much. I shall not necessarily be workin' against you, in the near future. In fact, our paths might cross somewhere in the Studley region!'

Wagoner sighed. He picked up the star, rolled its points round his palm and solemnly slipped it into the pocket of his coat. 'You'll be wantin' to ride off straight away?'

'As soon as I've had a bite to eat, Scott.'

'That being so, we'd better fry up some of that bacon.'

Between them, they put together a meal before parting.

11

No one else was taken into the confidence of the sheriff and Jeff Mays. Jeff was wearing that look which warned people not to ask questions when he brought his mount from the stable and halted it by the back door of the house.

He draped a blanket and saddled it most carefully, and hid his surprise when Scott came out with provisions and began to stuff them into his saddle-bags. When all was ready they shook hands. Jeff at once sprang into the saddle and urged his buckskin away from the buildings at a gentle trot.

Three or four men watched him from windows. It was a half-hour after dawn, and the sight of him going off alone occupied their minds while they expected Groves' party, long overdue.

Jeff kept up a brisk pace. He moved

due south down the valley, keeping to the west side of it and trying hard not to keep a special lookout behind him. He did not want to be followed, but he had to keep reminding himself that any real danger to him would come from the outlaws, and not from men who were jealous or angry with him among the posse riders.

His eyes were keen, in spite of the lump on his skull and the slight feeling of malaise which still bothered him from time to time. He spotted a high-flying eagle on one occasion. Another time he witnessed a squabble between a family of jays. Around nine o'clock two jack-rabbits chased one another across his line of ride, and made him wish he did not have to keep his presence so secret.

Besides, one of those in a stew would keep Mirabelle well fed for a day or so.

Shortly after that, he crested the rise on the west side of the valley and moved down the farther slope in search of the elusive dugout. The simple dwelling was one of the few unoccupied ones in the whole of the region which he knew about. He would not have used it as a hiding place had it not been remote. Now, for the first time, he wondered if he would have any difficulty in locating it again.

He had ridden this way towards it only once before, and now he could not remember enough of the earlier route to be sure that he was riding directly towards it.

The new terrain was a series of small hills, mostly capped by trees. Riding up and down them tired the buckskin and made it protest as Jeff goaded it along. No less than three hills had been investigated before he found the right one.

In fact, it was the horse which did the finding. It detected an almost imperceptible noise made by Mirabelle's mare, and that was sufficient to increase the pace and bring the meeting into being a little quicker.

The front, wooden wall of the dugout

remained undetected until Jeff was fifty yards away. Then he noticed a slight movement behind the window. The girl had recognised him. She came running out, her face flushed and her hair tied back behind her head in a ribbon.

She took the buckskin's head and Jeff slid down. He put an arm around her shoulders and kissed her in his brotherly fashion. 'How've you been, Mirabelle?'

'Oh, a little jumpy, Jeff, but all right, I guess. How have things been with you?'

'Exciting an' otherwise.' He thought back over all that had happened since he left her and rode into town with Ben Yerby's body. The girl linked her arm through his and drew him towards the house. Suddenly she noticed a small change in him.

'Your badge is gone! Did you take it down to hide your identity, or have you been dismissed?'

Mirabelle looked good and anxious. He studied her face, and wondered how the fates could bestow upon a heel like

Ben Yerby a woman with Mirabelle's qualities.

'No badge. I tossed it in. But a bump on the head I didn't ask for.'

In the doorway, Jeff whistled up the buckskin. He tethered it, and slackened the saddle on its back, while Mirabelle busied herself unloading the food.

'Somebody hit you, Jeff?'

He explained where he had come from, and how the ranch had been defended the previous night; how he thought Turkey must have hit him in an effort to get even, and then they were indoors and she was bathing his ugly bruise with clean cloth and hot water.

They drank a lot of coffee and she told him a whole lot more about her uneasy married life with Ben. Finally, she could see that he was tired, and that he did not plan a long stay.

'You still want to get clear of this area, Mirabelle?'

She nodded, elbows planted firmly on the table, green eyes studying every line of his face. 'Sure, I want to get clear. Not necessarily to a place a great distance away. I don't want to lose you again now you've come back into my life. Maybe if you could find me a place not associated with the outlaws I could make a decent livin' for myself, an' we could see each other regularly? How would that suit?'

'I guess that would suit me fine, Mirabelle, only I don't rightly know how to find such a place. Still, I do know a lot of people in Waterford, an' one or another of them ought to be able to help me when I go in to get the reward money.'

The mention of the bounty clouded Mirabelle's face again, but she fought a battle with her conflicting emotions and managed to produce a smile.

'You have the look of a man who wants to be on his way, cousin. Am I right?'

'Well, yes an' no.' Jeff fingered the dressing on his head lump. 'I don't rightly want to be separated from you, but I can't feel at ease while you're hidden away here over this side of the county. I've got to get you shifted an' the sooner the better.'

The girl leaned forward and gripped his hands. 'Jeff, is there anythin' else you haven't told me? You don't have to hold back because I'm a woman, or anythin'. After all, I'm proof against most kinds of shock now.'

Jeff blinked. He went over his earlier revelations. 'Well, there was a flurry of shots in the night. The deputies who were out ridin' hadn't got back when I left. Sis, is there anyone at all connected with Ben Yerby that you have affection for?'

Mirabelle's expression hardened. She shook her head. 'I kind of liked poor old Smithy, the cook, an' little Dan, the jack of all work, but I couldn't say that of any member of the gang. So, if you are tormentin' yourself on account of anythin' like that, Jeff, you don't have to. Jest one thing.'

'What thing, Mirabelle?'

'Don't go killin' jest for the sake of

killin', Jeff. If you ever do you won't be the same decent young fellow who grew up in my father's house. I like you the way you are. Uphold the law, if that's your kind of work, but don't bend the law to make killin' easy. No man is wholly bad.'

Jeff nodded. He saw the wisdom of his cousin's advice. He also saw the face of her parson father, Robert Jones, as he pronounced such words in his pulpit many years earlier.

'All right, sis, I'll bear that in mind. An' I won't be away long. Between us, we'll get things straightened out so that we can live more or less normally, like we used to do.'

Mirabelle pushed back her chair. She beamed at him.

'I'll look forward to that, Jeff. Now, you must go.'

★ ★ ★

In spite of his red hair, Red Richards was capable of great patience. He had shown it in the way in which he tracked Jeff to Mirabelle's hideout, and also by waiting for a full twenty minutes after the ex-deputy had departed before showing himself.

He had wandered around the top side of the hill in which the dugout was built, and was actually examining the grey mare when the startled girl heard him sneeze. She was out in no time at all and showing him the business end of a rifle from behind a tree.

'Step this way, mister, an' keep your hands well away from your body!'

Red expected her to react to the sneeze, but he had not seen her come. He smiled rather carefully and did as she suggested.

'I wasn't plannin' on stealin' the mare, if that's what you were thinkin'.'

'No, maybe not, but you did come along like a thief in the night, without showin' yourself or statin' your business, an' that ain't healthy in this part of the West, especially to a woman on her own. What *is* your business, mister?'

'If you're thinkin' I'm an outlaw, you can relax because I ain't, but I did come this way on account of the ex-deputy who's jest left. I go by the name of Red Richards, these days. It ain't the name I was christened, but it'll do for a casual acquaintance. My own name ain't one I'd be afraid to tell anyone, if I thought it would help.'

Mirabelle's lips were dry. As soon as she knew she had unwanted company, she had figured the stranger either for an outlaw, or for one of the posse. Maybe the man who had hit Jeff over the head.

'My name is . . . Mirabelle Drummond. I wonder, could you be the man who hit Jeff Mays over the head last night?'

Red flinched with surprise. He flinched at the name, Drummond, and also at the girl's accurate guess about Jeff's assailant. He knew then that she figured he'd come from the Yerby ranch. He kept the cause of his surprise to himself, and risked pointing a finger at the girl.

'I think Mays is protectin' you, an' that seems to suggest you have some connection with the Yerby outfit!'

Mirabelle sighed. She was growing tired of showing this stiff unyielding front, and the rifle was weighing down on her arms. She shifted her stance, threw a foot forward and pointed the weapon afresh.

'I sure do wish I could figure out what makes it *your* business, mister.'

'You couldn't be his wife, because you said your name was Drummond. But wait a bit. I've jest remembered something. There was that Circle D sign all over the ranch, an' that has to mean something. Maybe you can throw some light on the puzzle. Tell me, was the D sign at the Yerby place anything to do with the name Drummond?'

The girl's muscles were aching now. 'All right, so it stood for Drummond. An' a lot of good it will do you to know!'

Red was excited and still puzzled. 'Hey, I can see the way you are. Why don't you let me throw this side-iron away an' then we can talk easily. You'll find it hard to believe, but all I'm after is findin' my brother!'

He made a tentative move towards his gun belt. Mirabelle acted as though she was going to challenge the move, and then she thought better of it. She watched him toss the Colt aside and then lowered the muzzle of her rifle. Turning her back on him, she led the way to the front of the dugout, where she waited for him.

'All right, Mr Red Richards, you'd better come inside.'

Mirabelle pulled her chair away from the table and set it against a wall. Red did the same, setting his chair on the opposite side of the room.

'What is the name of your brother, Red?'

Her voice sounded dull, but not entirely devoid of interest.

'I don't know my brother, on account

of he left home before I was born — when my father married again! But I do know his name. He's Ben Drummond, an' Pa says he was nicknamed Blackie in his youth!'

Mirabelle's full lips became a round 'O'. 'Then your name is also Drummond! You are Red Drummond, or something of the sort!'

'Christened Richard Drummond, if it helps at all!'

'Let me get this straight! Are you claimin' to be Ben Yerby Drummond's kid brother? One he never knew because he'd left home before you were born?'

Red nodded slowly, and then shook his head. He was not at all sure of himself. In all this time it had never occurred to him that Ben Yerby could be the Ben Drummond he sought. How could it be?

He started to say something, faltered. 'An' you are — were Ben Yerby Drummond's wife?'

Mirabelle set her lips hard, nodding.

Already she was feeling sympathy for this man who had turned up out of nowhere and claimed to be kin by marriage. She wondered what sort of a man he was. Had he the same tendencies as Ben, for instance? What would his attitude to her be?

'Mrs Ben Drummond, the widow as of this week!'

'But — but that makes me your brother-in-law, Mrs Drummond, an' I ain't sure as how I like that on account of you've jest been entertainin' my brother's killer — if what you've told me is the truth!'

Red was finding the recent revelations hard to swallow.

'There's things I could tell you would make you feel a whole lot better about this mess, Red, if you're on the level. Tell me, is there any way in which you can prove who you are? I mean that you are Ben's brother?'

This request calmed Red down. He tossed his hat aside and fumbled out his tobacco sack, while he nodded and attempted to fit into place certain recent happenings which he had not properly understood. Mirabelle took the sack from him and made him a smoke.

'Sure, there is a way. I can prove it, all right. I'm wondering how we shall feel about one another when I say my piece. First off, there's one thing puzzlin' me. Were you, by any chance, the brown-haired young man who sent a message to Jeff Mays?'

'An' what if I was, Red?'

'Then you sent the earring which Turkey saw. Did — did Jeff give it back to you, Mrs Drummond?'

'Is that what you're after? Is that your angle? You want the emerald an' diamond earring my husband gave to me! Is that it?'

Mirabelle sounded hard, tired and a little cynical. Red perceived her mood. He was then quick to produce his own earring, and hold it up for her inspection. Her hands were a little unsteady when she produced the second trinket and held them together.

They were a beautifully matched pair.

'Why don't you wear them, Mrs Drummond? They'd bring out the fine green colour of your eyes!'

Mirabelle shrugged rather prettily. She pouted, blushed, and finally consented to fit them to her ear lobes, helped by a cracked mirror attached to a dirt wall.

'I think from now on you'd better call me Mirabelle. In some ways this meetin' has been as much a shock to me as it must have been to you. But there are other things you'll have to know, that is, if you've simply come lookin' for your kin, an' not to make trouble!'

Red did his best to reassure her. He smoked a second cigarette and asked about Jeff.

'So far as I know, Jeff Mays is my only livin' kin. He is my cousin, but he was brought up in my home as a brother. Hold on, I know how your thoughts must be runnin'. Jeff shot Ben because Ben wanted it that way. He had a bad accident with a half-wild stallion. The fall broke him up so that he was almost dead. He wanted Jeff to shoot him to get the reward money, you know, the bounty — '

Red staggered to his feet, knocking over the chair. 'Your cousin shot your husband! Is that what you're sayin'? For the reward money?'

Mirabelle rose at the same time, determined to be heard and to be believed. 'It was Ben's wish that *I* should have the reward money! Do you hear me? I couldn't have told Jeff to shoot Ben. Ben told him himself, as he was dyin'!'

Red subsided into his chair, almost knocking it over.

'You don't understand at all, an' I shouldn't have told you! It's my fault for bein' so frank with you,' the girl muttered. 'I was runnin' off at the mouth, that's all!'

She sat on her chair, draped an arm

over the back of it and laid her head on it. Although she made no sound, Red could tell she was crying by the way her shoulders shook.

'Sister-in-law,' he said, after an interval. 'I can see the way it is. But you've got to give me time to adjust. In jest a short time, I've found my brother, learned he was an outlaw. Now he's dead. An' I have a sister-in-law I didn't know anythin' about. Takin' it all at once is a little bit overwhelmin'.'

Mirabelle suggested. 'Maybe you ought to go away some place, an' come back when you've thought it all out, huh?'

He nodded, confessing to be sad and worried about Ben, but shyly telling of his pleasure at having a pretty sister-in-law.

'How will you feel towards Jeff, when you meet up with him?' the girl asked, in a matter-of-fact voice.

'All right, I suppose. If he can accept me for who I am I won't bear him any serious grudge. If he's plannin' on comin' out here with a substantial amount of money, he could need help, too. Tell me, *is* he comin' back here?'

She assured him that Jeff would be back, and with all the money. In an effort to cement the brittle alliance between them, she hunted out a photograph of Ben, taken several years ago, before he took to wearing his moustache.

Soon, he was ready to mount up again, and ride on, into town.

'Don't avoid Jeff,' Mirabelle suggested. 'Tell him I believe your story, an' that I accepted the other earring from you.'

Red thought it was good advice. He said as much, touched his hat and kneed his sorrel into action.

12

Around three o'clock that same after-noon, young Turkey was in the long bar of the Blue Horizon. He still looked a little pale, and out of sorts with himself. He had been in town for perhaps two hours and he felt as though he had little to celebrate even if he inherited the livery stable from his deceased friend, Baldy Peake.

As soon as Turkey realised that Jeff Mays had quit the Yerby ranch and his job, and that Red Richards had gone after him, the young man lost interest in what the sheriff and posse were trying to do. He had actually been in the act of explaining his own imminent departure when the riding group, bossed by Boris Groves, had slowly ridden back to the ranch with their dead man and wounded leader.

Wagoner had been deeply moved by

hearing details of the night clash. Turkey's whining had bothered him. He had turned on the youngster and insisted that he waited before going back to town, so that he could help with Groves and Peake's body.

Turkey calmed down. He waited long enough for Groves to be patched up and then accepted the responsibility for getting him, and Peake, back to town. One other rider had made the journey with him.

Peake had gone directly to the undertaker's slab. Groves had visited the doctor's, and Turkey paid a brief visit to the livery, manned only by a casual hand who did not want to stay on the job. After doing all that was necessary and leaving a scribbled message of advice for anyone who wanted to use the stables, Turkey turned to the important business of slaking his thirst and airing his current grievances.

He soon tired of hearing what a big turn-out there had been for the Yerby burial and raised his voice so that he would be heard. He gave a highly coloured account of everything that had happened since he teamed up with the posse, particularly the excitements of that morning when Jeff Mays had returned his badge and ridden off, and when Boris Groves' badly mauled party returned to the ranch with one dead.

'So you didn't actually see any action yourself, Turkey?' a farmer queried.

The young man agreed with this statement, but quickly covered his own possible loss of face with a description of the Yerby ranch and the kind of fittings the house had in it.

'It is true the livery will be yours, Turkey, now that Baldy's dead?' the barman asked, as he polished glasses.

'I believe that is so, Jamie, only I can't be certain till Lawyer Thomasson gets out the will an' reads it. I don't figure that will be today, though.'

The barman pushed another whisky along to Turkey and patted him on the shoulder. He winked at one of the nearest drinkers. 'We've got to look after young Master Turkey now, seein' as how he'll be a business man of substance from now on.'

'I don't see why Thomasson shouldn't tell you what's in store for you today, Turkey,' the farmer opined. 'After all, he ain't all that busy.'

Turkey drained his whisky glass and set it down on the bar with a bang. 'That's all you know, mister! Right now, he's busy with Jeff Mays who's collectin' the reward money for Ben Yerby. If you ask me, I'd say that sure was a fast pay-out, but then I don't have any experience of *that* sort of money comin' *my* way!'

Everybody in the West was interested in the paying out of reward money, although most of them never had any desire to earn it themselves.

Jamie, the barman, stroked his moustache and ran a hand over the black hair greased across his crown. Here was a good topic of conversation; something to keep the customers interested and affable.

'You mean to say that Mays is collectin' two thousand dollars in cash from Tom Thomasson, right at this minute?' he asked loudly.

'Go and see for yourself,' Turkey suggested. 'Jeff hasn't any other reason for dashin' along to see a lawyer that I know of. You all know Thomasson is empowered to pay rewards for the big companies! An' seein' as how he won't be in here to buy a free round of drinks, I'm thinkin' I'll be headin' back to the livery. Adios, amigos!'

The disconsolate young man was five yards from the batwings when Jamie Bates yelled after him. 'Hey, Turkey, you never did say whether you had any luck with the fellow who gave you the message for Jeff! You know, the one who put him on to Yerby!'

Turkey yawned. He turned briefly on his heel. 'No, I never did find the fellow. Maybe there's a good reason. I'm beginnin' to wonder if it mightn't have been a fellow at all!'

There was a gasp from those who heard, and Turkey, having stirred up the interest to a high degree, launched himself through the half-doors and into the street. He paused as the bright light attacked his eyes and moved with some reluctance towards the stable.

On the way, he saw Jeff May's buckskin tethered outside the lawyer's office, and that sight made him hasten his pace. Two men came out of the saloon shortly afterwards and had to make an effort to keep him in sight.

In the sheriff's swivel chair, Boris Groves, newly promoted to chief deputy, had sprawled with care, following a fresh patch-up of his wounds by the town doctor. He was smoking a cigar, and trying to make himself believe that he was enjoying his promotion when Red Richards appeared at the door, removed his hat and nodded.

'Take a seat, Red,' Groves offered. 'Say, you must have left the Yerby place not long after Jeff Mays. Is that right?'

'Yes, I only went along to the Yerby place with Turkey out of curiosity. How did your party make out?'

Groves worked the cigar around to the side of his mouth. He filled his lungs and told the story of the sudden shooting episode with plenty of embellishments, making much out of his admonishment of Peake, after the liveryman was dead. At last, he ran out of breath, and his curiosity about Red made him dry up.

'Tell me, what brought you to town, Red?'

'Well, you could say I'm jest a plain wanderer, Deputy, an' then again another sort of answer would be that a sorrel gelding brought me. But that wouldn't be the right sort of answer. If you pressed me, I'd admit to havin' been interested in seein' Ben Yerby. But now he's planted, so I figured the next best thing was to come along here an' ask to see a reward notice. Do you have such a thing?'

Groves hauled open the drawer

where the notices were usually kept. For a minute or more he looked in vain, and then he remembered that he had done away with the Yerby notice as soon as he had entered the office. It was in the waste-paper basket. He leaned sideways and fished it out.

'Here you are, pardner, I'd forgotten we'd done with it. Have it, if it's any use to you.'

Red grinned. He took the crumpled notice and sat down on the edge of a chair to examine it. It showed a full-face photograph of the wanted man without a moustache. Yerby's expression in the photograph was harsher than when he had posed for Mirabelle's picture, but there was no doubt that it was the same man.

Red permitted himself a moment's reverie, wondering if his father had ever really known that his older son was an outlaw. Perhaps he had kept Ben's second name, Yerby, from Red because of some secret knowledge, or perhaps he had never really known what Ben had done with his life.

A smile played at the corner of his lips as he thought how old Doc Drummond would have approved of his daughter-in-law. At that point, his resolve to do all he could for Mirabelle grew. Because of her he would have to ally himself to Jeff. This far, he had not taken the girl's advice and sought out the ex-deputy. He had a feeling that Jeff might be too absorbed in his present endeavours to want the close comradeship of a comparative stranger: especially when he learned that Red had hit him over the head with a gun specially to search him for an earring.

Red licked his lips. He became aware that Groves' attention was on him.

He said: 'Nobody could claim Yerby was a handsome hombre, could they?'

Groves shook his head. 'Nope, I guess not. They lead ugly lives an' they end up ugly as sin. Don't go studyin' it too closely in case you end up that way yourself.'

Red laughed. He stood up, thanked

Groves for the notice and moved out into the street. He saw by a quick glance up the street that Jeff's buckskin was outside the lawyer's office. His first job on hitting town had been to visit the barber's shop. There he had had his chin scraped and his hair trimmed.

Now, he slipped into the Chinaman's place and ordered a plate of ham and eggs for a man in a hurry. The little Oriental went into his act with the frying pan and Red slumped into a chair. He hoped he would not miss Jeff through pausing for food.

$$\star \quad \star \quad \star$$

Lofty Rington and Jack Whale had the knack of blending in with the landscape when they did not want to be noticed. In the Blue Horizon Turkey had not noticed them at all. When they reached the livery, he was seeing them for the first time.

Lofty was tall, bandy and muscular. Beer drinking and the lack of walking exercise had provided him with a small unwanted paunch. He had small pointed ears which stuck out like flaps and tousled brownish hair which looked as if it had not been washed or combed in all his thirty-six years.

Jack Whale, by contrast, was only about average in height. He was in his early forties. The whites of his bulbous grey eyes were flecked with tiny red veins. His face was badly pockmarked. The hair was trimmed close all over the top of his head, as well as on his face.

Whale nudged his companion as they spotted Turkey through a window, resting his weight on the handle of a broom and looking around him in rather a disconsolate fashion.

'You know how we planned it, Lofty. Rub him up the right way, first. But don't take too long about it, eh?'

Together, they passed through the door in the middle of the wide doorway and paused, grinning at Turkey as though he was a long-lost friend.

'Howdy, amigo, I figure we put our

animals in here while you were still out hitting the trail some place. If you've been ridin' hard you won't feel like pushin' a broom around. Why don't you give that over to Lofty, here? He's a great one with a broom. Besides, it'll give you time to make out our bill, 'cause we're figurin' on leavin' town real soon.'

Rington took the broom and went to work with it. Turkey smiled and allowed himself to be led into the office, which had a window opening on to the street. He took for the feed and the use of the stalls, held the money for a moment or two, and then thrust it into his pocket.

Whale noted this. He then pointed down the street to where Jeff's horse was still waiting. 'That'd be the ex-deputy's cayuse, I'm thinkin',' he murmured. 'Likely to be a well-to-do fellow when he comes out of there, I shouldn't wonder.'

'Two thousand bucks, if I remember rightly,' Turkey responded. 'A goodly sum for a short piece of risky work put

189

into his hands by another fellow.'

Whale took a swig of whisky out of a flat bottle. He handed it to Turkey just as the latter became aware of it. Turkey wiped off the mouth of the bottle and tilted a good tot down his throat. It made him cough as he swallowed but Whale did not appear to notice.

'Turkey, if I was you, I'd go after that hombre an' force him to part with a share of the loot he's made out of the Yerby shootin'. You may not get another chance like this as long as you live. Do you believe me?'

The earnest, pockmarked face very close to his own startled Turkey at first, but Whale wore his most ingenuous expression, and as the whisky went to work the visage seemed less and less repelling.

Turkey said, 'Jeff is a pretty good shot with a gun. I've got two burns on my body now to bear witness to how accurate he is. I don't know if I'd want to risk goin' after him again.'

'All the more reason why you

should,' put in Lofty Rington, who, having just completed his chore, entered the smaller room. 'If you wear his scars then he surely does owe you somethin'. An' if you're worried about goin' after him to er — persuade him, well you don't have to, because Jack an' me, we'd be glad to go along an' see you get fair play! Now, what do you say to that?'

They gave Turkey more whisky. In ten minutes he was almost prepared to go along to the lawyer's office and stake his claim there. It was not too hard to dissuade him, however, and Whale occupied him by having him write out another notice saying he would be out of town for a day.

Meanwhile, Lofty collected the clay-bank and the bay gelding along with Turkey's pinto and tethered them all in the alley alongside the building.

Jeff came out of Thomasson's office after a protracted stay. Most of that time, the lawyer had simply been chatting with him while the confidential clerk had been along to the saddler's shop and purchased a leather money belt especially to take away the dollar bills of high denomination.

When eventually Jeff emerged on to the street he was wearing the leather belt around his waist a little higher than his ordinary belt. It had two pouches, each holding fifty twenty-dollar bills, and he hoped it did not look too conspicuous under his leather vest.

He gave the street a long careful scrutiny in all directions and took ample time to ensure that no one was paying any special attention to his movements. One or two people looked him over, but the ones he saw were ordinary townsfolk doing their shopping and day-to-day chores.

When he forked the buckskin and gave it its most valuable load to date, he was as certain as any man could be that he was taking no one after him.

Whale and Rington, both well versed in following their fellow men, kept well out of sight with their mounts and also with Turkey until Jeff had ridden clear of town. Then, and only then, did they permit the young man to come out into Main Street, mount his pinto and show them the way.

The two riding partners, who were keen to have the proceeds of Jeff's belt for themselves, could, of course, have made the pursuit without Turkey's assistance, but they had brought him along for one special purpose. They thought that by using him they would leave their own future a little more secure.

Turkey indulged in short noisy bursts of singing as they rode out of town towards the west in the wake of the ex-deputy. This habit soon had Jack Whale secretly grimacing and was the reason why they stayed farther behind their quarry than was normally necessary in this kind of pursuit.

They were well past Two Mile Rock and far from any well-established trails when Jack yawned. He slipped his canteen off his saddle horn and generously provided a drink for all three. Next, he turned his attention to Lofty.

'How are your fingers, amigo? I'm feelin' like a nice smoke, an' I'm sure our friend Turkey is, too. So how about it?'

Lofty tweaked one of his flap-like ears, raised his brows and nodded. 'All right, pardner, if you want a smoke, a smoke you shall have.'

Turkey, riding between them, marvelled at the dexterity of the tall man. In no time at all, he had fashioned three smokes. One was passed across to Jack. Turkey took the second one, and Lofty placed the third behind his ear.

Jack obliged by pulling a matchstick out of his hat band and rasping it into flame with his thumbnail. Turkey and Lofty moved closer. Turkey bent over Jack's cupped hands to get his smoke lit, and it was exactly at that moment that Lofty's long thin-bladed knife appeared. The blade was driven between the youngster's ribs and into his heart before he knew a thing about it.

Lofty withdrew the blade and then took back the cigarette which was sticking to Turkey's upper lip. In withdrawing the blade, Lofty pushed hard on the body and Turkey slowly spilled out of his saddle, Jack having grabbed for him and missed him.

13

A single low moan escaped the lips of the dying youth as his body hit the trail and his hat cartwheeled away. Whale had control of the pinto, but his eyes showed anything but satisfaction.

'Doggone it, Lofty, you're gettin' careless these days!'

'But I stabbed him clean as a whistle an' he never knew what had happened!'

'All that is so, but you didn't have to tip him on the trail like that! We could have taken him a little farther along with us an' selected a good place. After all, we want it to look good if anyone is ever to believe the ex-deputy murdered him.'

Lofty massaged his jaw with the palm of his hand. He was impatient and he had ridden with Whale long enough not to bother hiding it.

'Well?' he queried. 'He's still down

there, do we get down an' haul him up again, or simply move him aside? I'm more interested in that jasper up ahead. Men have gotten away from us before today because we've let too much space get between us!'

'All right, I'll get him,' Whale conceded.

He had swung his leg out of leather and was about to put a boot on the ground when Lofty ordered him to be silent. After restraining the horses they both listened hard. Lofty was certain, and Whale felt fairly sure that another rider was coming after them. The reactions of the three horses seemed to confirm it, too.

'Well?' Lofty asked again. 'Do we get into the bushes an' shoot this hombre off our tail, or do we press on an' try an' catch the man with the money?'

'It's good to tell which way your thoughts are,' Whale jeered, 'the only thing that really makes you keen is the jingle of money or the smell of bills. So all right, we'll leave him here an' make tracks after Mays. The fellow who's behind us may not be interested in us, or Mays' reward. Let's go!'

So saying, Whale slung his leg back over the saddle and started his bay gelding forward, towing the pinto along behind him.

Less than five minutes after Turkey had died, Red Richards arrived at the spot and hurriedly dismounted. He checked for a heart beat and also for signs of a pulse, but found neither. Turkey being stabbed to death like that made Red watchful. It also made him wary on behalf of Jeff, who could not be far in front of the killers.

As he slipped out his rifle, Red felt pleased that he had seen the two strangers setting out with Turkey, otherwise he might have been tempted to believe that Jeff had prevented Turkey from following him a second time. It would have been hard to believe, though, that a man with Jeff's background would stoop to such cold-blooded killing.

Putting the weapon to his shoulder, Red fired two bullets into the air. He hoped that Jeff would hear them and be warned, but he did not expect to hear a return gunshot because that would have put the strangers more closely in touch with him.

Jeff was within easy earshot. He heard and understood the nature of the rifle shots, and although he was puzzled as to who had fired the weapon, he increased his pace and did everything he knew to cut out detours on the way to the dugout.

The next pair, who had already lost ground when Turkey was despatched, made a couple of small errors in following the sign. Consequently, they lost track of Jeff and spent a great deal of time reviling one another while they tried unsuccessfully to trace his route again.

Mirabelle was taking her ease under trees with a hat resting gently on her face when she heard her name called repeatedly.

She stuck the hat on her head, ran indoors for her rifle, and presented herself fifty yards down the slope in front of the dugout with the weapon at the ready. Jeff swept towards her on his sweating animal with his jaw set hard.

The girl felt her chest constrict. Her heart thumped. 'Why, what is it, Jeff? Are you in trouble? Where's Red? Is there somebody followin' you?'

'There's somebody in back of me, all right, sis, but I don't know who it is! A short while ago somebody fired two warnin' rifle shots! Search me if I know who it is, but you've got to get your things together an' move out, *muy pronto!* Hear me?'

'I hear you, Jeff, but you're plumb tuckered out. You'll need a rest before you can go on again. By the way, did you get the money?'

Jeff dismounted and patted the belt around his waist. 'It's here all right, but who's the Red you were speakin' of? I didn't meet anybody on trail. Should I have done?'

Mirabelle chuckled as she led him hurriedly back to the dugout. 'That would have been Red Richards, better know as Richard Drummond, my brother-in-law. He was up at Ben's place when you were there. Turkey took him along. He didn't answer when I asked if he'd hit you over the head, but I guess he did it. He was lookin' for the earring, you know. His father gave him one, an' the one Ben gave me made a pair. Here, see them both together!'

'Are you tellin' me this Red is not an outlaw? That he came lookin' for his brother an' he doesn't mind what I had to do to get the reward for you?'

'I'm tellin' you jest that, cousin. He was hostile at first, but when I explained how things came about, he began to see everythin' in perspective. Anyways, he's friendly now. You've got yourself an ally, if you want one. Maybe a rival even, for lookin' after the Widow Drummond, I mean!'

'Friendly or not, we've got to travel. An' if all's true you tell me about this

Red fellow, he's a better tracker than any Indian I ever met. He'll catch up with us, all right, if he still wants to.'

A half-hour of brisk banter and eating went by while Mirabelle acted as guard. Soon Jeff pronounced himself ready to travel again, and it was the girl who was the more watchful as they left the dugout behind and made tracks across country towards the north-east.

Although they were watchful, the pair saw no one before it was time to make camp and bed down. They chose a spot above a shallow stream in a narrow draw. Jeff arranged that they should sleep rough for that first night. Red had not shown up, and neither had the men from whom he was trying to protect them.

Mirabelle was hidden protectively between the mare and the buckskin a good thirty yards away from the flickering light of the fire. Two bundles, one on either side, built on saddles, gave the appearance of two campers huddled near the blaze. Jeff was twenty yards away, lying prone behind a fallen tree, a vantage point which enabled him to see in all directions as far as visibility permitted.

Red tossed a stone into the small clearing and had his first inkling that the bundles were not as innocent as they seemed when neither of them moved.

'Hey, Jeff, are you there?'

His voice was quiet, but Jeff heard it. 'Name yourself!'

'Red Richards, or if you prefer it, Dick Drummond. You'll know now that Mirabelle kept my earring. I hope you believe I'm on your side.'

Mirabelle was also listening now, but she kept quiet.

'Tell me what happened on trail this afternoon,' Jeff requested, without committing himself.

'Two strangers, outlaws I suppose, came out of town with Turkey, followin' you up close. They must have tired of his conversation because one of them stabbed him to death. I found Turkey's body jest before I fired the warning shots.'

'Thank you. Any further sign of the outlaws? Do you know why they brought Turkey?'

'I think they've lost you. You must have increased your speed after the shootin'. It's hard to tell why they brought him along. I guess they may have figured to use him against you in some way. Who can read the mind of a killer?'

Jeff yawned. Red stayed close and watchful, but no one happened to threaten their lives, or to disturb their rest. At breakfast, the three came together for the first time and ironed out one or two existing differences.

Jeff reiterated that as soon as he had put Mirabelle into a safe place he was going to ride against the gang, members of which had made her life hard in the past. He showed a note of commendation from the Wells, Fargo agent which impressed Red.

'Why did you take down your badge,

Jeff, if you intended to go on fightin' against the Yerby gang?' Richards asked.

'Because the way I wanted to work I couldn't be wholly frank with old Scott Wagoner, the sheriff. I'm goin' to do my best to break up this whole gang, an' when they're scattered, or locked up, or under the soil, maybe I'll go back an' ask for the badge again. But I can't go against what I've jest said. That gang has been terrorisin' this territory far too long!'

'I like a man who knows his own mind,' Red commented. 'As it happens, I see things in a similar way. I've lost my brother. I don't want to lose touch with my sister-in-law. I'll do what I can to help you hunt these renegades down, Jeff. That is, if you feel you can work with another man around.'

Jeff mused over the offer for a while and finally shook hands.

That day, they rode steadily towards Studley, a place south-east of Waterford which in recent years had grown prosperous due to the railroad passing through it. Mirabelle was content to hum to herself for much of the riding time. She was puzzled about one thing, but Jeff cleared it up during the afternoon.

'The last thing Ben said to me was to watch Studley, because there might be a strike there. Now you, Red, might think it strange me takin' Mirabelle towards Studley, a place where her enemies might be. But it ain't all that strange, because we ain't takin' her right into Studley.

'We're headin' for a place a few miles this side, a tiny community known as Freighter's Ford. It'll turn out for the best, you'll see.'

The person recommended by Tom Thomasson as likely to take a young woman in for a while was a parson's wife, known in Freighter's Ford as Mrs Reverend. Around four that same afternoon, Jeff doffed his hat just back from the flower-hung porch of the neat detached log dwelling and made himself known to the parson's wife.

She was a small, energetic person with a broad nose and ample jaw. Her eyes were blue and very bright, and the fingers of her broad hands were forever working while she listened to Jeff's explanation.

A neat cotton blouse went well with a black full skirt. Her long greying hair was parted down the middle and pinned in a bun at the nape of her neck.

'Yes, yes, yes,' she replied, at length. 'Well, it is true we take in a guest or two now and again. But they have to be recommended, an' your Mr Thomasson only recommends the best people. So it's this young lady, is it, who needs a shelter over her head for a short while?'

'Yes, ma'am, Mrs Mirabelle Drummond. She's a widow, in fact. An' she wants time to get over her bereavement. My friend, here, and I will be in Studley quite a bit in the near future, but we'd like to call on Mrs Drummond now an' again, if we may.'

Mrs Reverend ushered the two men into her sitting room and gave them coffee while she chatted to Mirabelle and showed her her private bedroom. Reasonable terms were quickly agreed, and Jeff stood up when the older woman started asking if they wanted a meal.

'No, no ma'am, as I told you we've business in Studley, an' as we want to get there without any sort of delay, we'll leave Mrs Drummond in your good hands an' finish the rest of our journey.'

Mrs Reverend accepted this. She shook hands with the men and permitted them a minute or two on their own to say their farewells to Mirabelle.

'You'll call on me often,' the girl enjoined them. 'Think of my nerves if I don't hear from you for a long time.'

Jeff promised. He kissed her cheek and Red followed up by kissing her hand. As they rode out of sight, Jeff began to see what Mirabelle meant when she described Red as a rival.

At a little after five o'clock they were received by Town Marshal Ira Lumb into his office. He was a tall, stooping man of forty-seven with long tobacco-stained gapped teeth and a permanent frown which suggested he had liver trouble. Tufty greyish-white hair stood out around the edges of a big-brimmed grey hat and a flapping vest of the same colour masked his black shirt.

Even his stoop did not conceal his six feet three inches as he beckoned his visitors to take a chair. In the background, his nephew, Joe, hovered. Joe Lumb was just twenty-one and he was very proud to be his uncle's deputy. He had levelled off at five feet eleven inches; a thick-shouldered young man with a lantern jaw and short, wiry black hair.

There was an air of excitement in the office even before the visitors arrived. The marshal explained it: 'Seems we're due for a little action, gents. Sheriff Wagoner an' his posse stopped the southbound stage from Sutler's Creek earlier in the day. They gave the shotgun guard a carefully worded message. An' as if that wasn't enough, we had a telegraph message worded by the sheriff from the office in Sutler's Creek. Message put in by a fellow named Burgh. Rex Burgh.'

Jeff grinned and winked at Red. He said: 'You'll have noticed I'm not wearin' my badge any more, Ira. I've handed it in for a while, on account of the private war against the Yerby gang maybe callin' for irregular methods of fightin'.

'I'm still on the side of the law, though. In case you doubt it I had Thomasson pen out this letter for you. You'll see he still has confidence in me.'

The marshal chuckled when he had read the note. 'How you fight outlaws is your business, Jeff. If there's anythin' I can do to help, I'll be only too pleased. An' that goes for my nephew, Joe, as well. Accordin' to what I've learned by the message and the telegraphed note, Scott is expectin' action here in Studley.

'Apart from tellin' me he's convergin' on the town, he wants to keep the presence of his posse a secret. I can tell you, though, that he's goin' to make directly for the Studley Minin' Company, an' that anyone who wants to see him in a hurry will have to look in that direction. Anythin' else I can tell you?'

'Is there any special reason why anyone should attempt a hold-up in this town, right now, Ira?' Jeff asked.

'None that I know of, Jeff. But I'll be watchin' an' listenin' an' I suppose you'll keep in touch.'

Jeff nodded, and stood up. 'Sure as fate, Ira.' He perceived that Red was pointing towards the money belt. 'By the way, do you happen to have a strong safe around here?'

'One of the best in town, although it ain't generally known, Jeff. An' no charge for usin' it.'

Jeff then surrendered the belt, which he explained was the property of a young lady lodging with the Mrs

Reverend at Freighter's Ford. Lumb asked for no further information, and when the belt was locked away the two visitors said their thanks and left.

They rode back to Freighter's Ford after buying some victuals and made a camp within a furlong of the parson's house. Neither of them sought to make contact with Mirabelle, but they kept the house under observation from time to time.

Some time after sundown, a single horse started to make its way towards the small community. Red, who was finding it hard to settle, picked up his rifle and went a little closer to the trail to see who it was.

'You'll never believe who *that* was,' he murmured, on his return.

Jeff waited for him to tell, and when he explained that it was Mrs Reverend the fair man whistled in surprise. The parson's wife was at least forty-five and the way she behaved up at the house had suggested that she was far too demure for horseback riding in a pair of men's pants.

The knowledge that she was tougher than the men had expected helped them to sleep without fears on Mirabelle's behalf.

14

During the next day, Jeff and Red posted themselves in useful places of observation where they could study the kind of traffic which came and went on the trails which served Studley. To the north-west was Waterford; to the north was Sutler's Creek. A long and very old trail came from the west, out of the very heart of Arizona territory, located not very far from the railroad. This one passed through Studley, and carried on eastwards until it linked up with the border between two hill plateaux.

There was another trail coming up from the south, but that one escaped observation by the partners because Jeff felt sure that the various members of the Yerby gang were located north of the roalroad line.

Freight wagons, farmers' carts, buggies and buckboards came and went; so did stagecoaches, used mostly by people who wanted to link up with the railroad. There were horse caravans, too, and many a single rider churning up the dirt on his own.

The watchers made very good use of the glass, and where they were the least suspicious they came out of hiding and engaged men in conversation, but at the end of the day they could not honestly say that they had observed a person who was obviously an outlaw.

It was a fruitless day. Towards the end of it, they rode past Mrs Reverend's house a couple of times to give Mirabelle the idea that they were still close and interested in her. But they did not make contact. Rightly or wrongly, they judged that she would be resting and getting over the worst of her grieving for the husband who had been taken from her so suddenly.

The next day they went into town. Red would have been content to further their examination of faces as on the previous day, but Jeff wanted to be more thorough. He started to tackle the investigation from the angle of what the outlaws were likely to steal.

There were no less than three banks with a branch in Studley. One of them, a small local bank, had been there before the railway came. The other two had been built shortly afterwards. One, in particular, belonging to the South-Western Territories Banking Association, had prospered considerably. Its long half-brick, half-timber building accounted for just over half the banking business done in the town.

For no particular reason, Jeff presented his letter of commendation to the manager of the South-Western Territories bank last. He asked the small, dapper manager the same questions which he had asked in the other two. He wanted to know if there was any big shipment of money or valuables due which renegades might take an unhealthy interest in.

Jasen, the manager of the South-Western, talked around the subject for a while. When he had satisfied himself beyond doubt that Jeff and Red were on the level, and not just lookout men for the type of organisation they were fighting, he began to open up.

He revealed that considerable funds were being brought from the bank's branch in Sutler's Creek that very day; funds which were to be housed in his bank. All the time he was talking, Jeff had the feeling that the manager was not being wholly frank, but at least he was telling them something. He further revealed the times at which the money was being moved, and authorised his two visitors to go along the trail towards Sutler's Creek and make contact with Major Dunlap, who was in charge of a special bunch of outriders charged with keeping the money safe.

Within half an hour of contacting Manager Jasen, the two partners were mounted up and pushing their mounts up the north trail in search of bank funds and almost certain trouble. Two hours of hard riding, however, brought them to the coach in which the funds were being shifted.

They found the Major a little out of sympathy with their self-imposed task, and came back as extra guards without having achieved anything useful. By three-thirty in the afternoon, they were sitting their weary horses within fifty yards of the bank while certain leather packages were transferred from the treasure box under the driver's seat to the vaults of the bank.

Marshal Ira Lumb appeared beside them without their having noticed his approach.

'Well, gents, by the condition of your hosses I'd say you surely were puttin' yourselves out. Only this far, you don't seem to have made much progress. I always feel better when I see that shipment goin' in safely through the bank doors.'

Jeff passed the time of day, but he had little by way of conversation to offer. This far, in his private investigations, he had made little progress — as the marshal had pointed out — and he was not far from admitting himself baffled.

The only concern of any size worthy of the attentions of a large renegade group, other than the banks, was the Studley Mining Company, located a few miles to the south-east. This was one place which Jeff had never considered looking into because he had definite knowledge that Scott Wagoner and the balance of his posse had gone through to the mine area on the offchance of a strike there.

The marshal remarked: 'By the way, Jeff, your lady friend didn't stay long at the Reverend's place.'

This observation really startled the two tired riders out of their misery. Lumb repeated his statement for Red.

He added: 'Mrs Reverend came through on the buckboard this afternoon, an' a presentable young woman was ridin' with her. Of course I could be wrong. In any case, it ain't nothin' to do with me, gents.'

The business of transfer outside the bank came to an end. Jeff and Red drifted up the street with the marshal beside them. They had to move out to accommodate a freight cart at one place, and Ira called out to the driver. The freighter, who called regularly at the parson's residence, confirmed that there was only the one young woman, tall with dark brown hair, staying at the place.

He touched his hat and they moved on again, slightly more baffled than before.

Jeff remarked: 'I expect Ira, here, is as baffled as we are, knowin' as he does that we have Mirabelle's money in his safe.' He turned to the marshal again. 'Tell me, Ira, does Mrs Reverend often go off on the buckboard, or ridin' alone an' wearin' man's pants?'

The last suggestion stopped Marshal Lumb in his walk.

'I thought you boys knew a whole lot about Mrs Reverend before you rode out these ways,' he observed.

Jeff shrugged, and Red looked rather uneasy.

'I don't believe you do!' the marshal went on. 'Well, the fact is the Reverend sees his parish as bein' a whole lot bigger than the town of Studley. So he makes up his mind where he's a-goin' to evangelise next an' then he sets off. Sometimes there's things he wants. He don't always come back for them, though. He sends messages to Mrs Studley along with anyone who happens to be comin' near Freighter's Ford, an' she figures out a way to get them to him.

'As often as not, she gets out the buckboard, puts what he wants on it an' rides out for miles an' miles till she finds him. She's good an' tough is Mrs Reverend!'

Lumb started to fumble inside his vest for his tobacco sack. By the time he had his hand on it, one of his listeners had dismounted on either side of him. Red was too excited to defer to Jeff this time.

He asked: 'Marshal, did you say the Mrs Reverend's proper name was Mrs Studley, or was it a slip of the tongue?'

'I thank you for listenin' so hard, gents, but it was no slip of the tongue. Everyone in these parts knows the Reverend Studley is referred to simply as the Reverend on account of his surname is the same as this town's name. An' the same goes for Mrs Reverend, too. Say, you ain't goin' to tell me you never knew that — an' you comin' into town as special investigators!'

Jeff suddenly became anxious. Without knowing quite why he was so disturbed, he took his leave of the marshal, and, closely followed by Red, he started a race to the house of the Reverend, fearing that in some clever way Mirabelle's enemies had managed to get control of her movements. Otherwise, why would she want to go off driving with the parson's wife without leaving any messages?

A brief chat with two male lodgers, observers from the west coast, confirmed that Mrs Reverend had left the house several hours earlier with Mrs Drummond and that they were not expected back that night. The younger and more observant of the two visitors, when pressed, admitted to having seen a bag put aboard the buckboard with Mrs Drummond's things in it. The younger woman had also looked a trifle put out.

And that was that. All they could do was to ask that Mrs. Drummond left a message at the marshal's office in town, in the event that she returned unexpectedly.

After giving the horses a brief rub down, they walked them back into Studley still feeling slightly disturbed. They partook of a quick meal in an eating house and then went along to the hotel next to the big bank. Sheer nagging curiosity made Jeff ask where the driver and guard of the all-important coach could be located, and that threw the hotel receptionist into a fit of coughing.

The fellow left the reception desk, peered into the lounge, and suggested that they should ask the same question of Mr Jasen, the bank manager, who was taking his ease in there.

Jasen looked slightly abashed as they came in, covered in dust. He offered them a seat and some coffee, while he finished his meal. They removed their hats and squatted on the edge of chairs rather gingerly.

'Now see here, Mr Jasen,' Jeff began, 'we didn't come into this buildin' to interrupt your meal. All we asked out there was a perfectly simple question as to where I could locate the crew of the coach which brought the funds from Sutler's Creek. The clerk sent us to you. Now, what's the mystery?'

Jasen tucked his napkin a little more firmly into the neck of his shirt. 'Well, gentlemen, you came into town anxious to help an' to do the banks a bit of good. I don't see that it will do any harm to say where the coach crew is located. At least, not to yourselves. The fact is, the coach has driven on through, not to carry passengers in the ordinary way, but to deliver the mine payroll, which is due today.'

Jasen gave his information glibly and confidently, but Jeff had a growing premonition that this was the sort of happening which would most interest a ruthless gang of raiders with a shrewd leader.

'Major Dunlap an' his outriders,' Red commented, 'they'll still be ridin' with the payroll, of course?'

Jasen lost some of his colour. 'Er, well, no. They aren't, as a matter of fact. After makin' the big show of guardin' the coach an' funds all the way from Sutler's Creek, we felt certain that the outlaws who might be interested would think *all* valuables had been unloaded here in town. We felt certain, therefore, that the payroll would be safe.'

He glanced round the room to see if any of the other diners had overheard the gist of his revelations. None had, but the expressions on the faces of his companions killed what was left of his appetite.

'Perhaps you have later information. Have the outlaws been reported on the way to the mine?'

There was a scraping of chair legs on the floor as the two dusty riders rose to their feet and prepared to leave the room. In the foyer they paused, still trying to figure out how a determined gang would make their strike in these circumstances.

Jasen followed them into the foyer, his table napkin still tucked into his shirt. 'You think we have blundered? I hope you are wrong. A month's pay for that mine amounts to many thousands of dollars. Tell me, is it too late to put matters right?'

'I think you'd better come along with us to the marshal's office. We'll be better able to tell if it's too late or not when we've seen a detailed map an' asked his advice!'

They walked their horses to the peace office, and still Jasen found it hard to keep up. Red squinted up at the sun. He knew the hour to be about five in the afternoon. He was thinking that this day could be showdown day with the Yerby outfit.

Jeff's eyes were closed down to pin-head size. He was seeing again Ben Yerby's last moments of life. The way the finger went across the throat when he had warned about watching Studley. He could have meant a noose around the neck; or a knife across the throat; or even a parson's collar which goes across the front of a man's neck without a break!

15

The partners stood either side of the peace office door and almost launched Jasen in ahead of them. Red held back for a few seconds: 'Jeff, some time soon we ought to telegraph Waterford about Turkey not comin' back. They ought to know I buried him. Besides, that livery will be crawlin' with hosses.'

As soon as they were in the office, Jeff scribbled out the message for Waterford on a pad. He had finished before Jasen started to open up about the new development in shifting money. Jasen's reluctance to talk about it stemmed from the fact that the marshal had not been told about the payroll going on to the mine.

'Something's happened,' the lawman observed tentatively, one big boot resting on the seat of his chair.

'Ira, will you get out the best map of

the area you have? We want to study the lie of the land between town an' the mine. For your information the mine payroll has been sent on by coach without the escort.'

Lumb snorted, set his jaw, and quickly shifted his hostile expression from the bank manager to his nephew, who was standing poker-faced and alert by the street window.

'Joe, get me the big map,' the marshal ordered.

They spread it out between them, and for a few seconds mutual embarrassment was forgotten while the details were studied. The railway track from Studley to the New Mexico border had the shape of a taut bow, being a curve over a straight line running east-west. The old trail, covering the same territory, was below the railway line like the slack string of a bow. Some five or six miles east of the town a side track went off to the south, heading directly to the mine basin which was between two and three miles from the fork. A secondary track was marked from Studley to the mine which could reduce the minimum distance between the two places to a little over six miles. The secondary track, however, was not recommended for carts or wheeled vehicles of any kind. All it was really suitable for was a man on a horse.

Jeff cleared his throat. 'Ira, certain revelations today have made some of us look like fools. I believe that the mine payroll may be in grave danger. Something Ben Yerby said when he died makes me think this. Now, do you feel you could give us maximum help in an effort to put things right before it's too late?'

'Well,' Lumb returned guardedly, 'Mr Jasen there is one of the leadin' townsmen, an' he seems to be thinkin' the same way as you are. I reckon the answer is 'yes'.'

They all nodded. Deputy Joe moved nearer.

Jeff went on: 'I want somebody to contact Major Dunlap an' have him take his outriders along to the fork in the trail at the highest speed possible. If he could get there without actually followin' the trail, I think we'd stand a better chance of safeguardin' the money.'

'I'll see to that myself,' Jasen promised, 'jest as soon as you've fully outlined your plan, Mr Mays.'

'Good. My pardner here, an' me, we'll go right after the coach an' see what can be done in that direction. Then we need to alert the sheriff. Somebody who can ride fast an' is absolutely trustworthy has to tell him the way we figure things. Also remind him not to overlook the obvious way to the border. He'll know what is meant.

'An' lastly, a word to you, Ira. If Mrs Drummond comes back through town on any pretext whatever, ask her on my behalf to break all existin' arrangements an' stay somewhere close in town until she has contacted me, personally. Is that understood?'

The marshal's mind was busy with

the possible implications behind this last instruction. He refrained from asking questions, however, and at once directed his nephew, Joe, to collect the two fastest horses available and use them in an all-out gallop to contact the sheriff near the mine.

Joe went up the street three minutes later while Jeff and Red were still watering their horses at the nearest trough. Jasen called to them as they mounted up from a building some fifty yards away. He intimated that he had made contact with the Major and that the bank guards would be on their way almost immediately.

'Well, pardner, this is it,' Jeff murmured. 'Are you sure you want to stick your neck out for a sister-in-law you've only jest met?'

Red nodded and grinned. 'Sure. I'd like to take my chance to kill the Yerby tag once an' for all!'

Side by side they cantered up the street with the tall marshal looking thoughtfully after them.

About the same time, the Reverend Studley's buckboard was pulled up in a stationary position on the flattened ground alongside of the railroad track, on the south side. This ground was not really a trail at all, but in preparing the ground for the steel rails the railroad gangers had levelled it and made it passable for wheeled vehicles.

Two dun horses were out of the shafts and cropping grass about seventy yards back from the rails, the grass which had grown closer to the rails having been burned away by wood smoke from passing locomotives. Mrs Reverend was dangling her legs from the box and looking down rather glumly towards a small fire which was taking a long time to boil the coffee pot.

Mirabelle was nowhere in sight. This was deliberate because she had hidden herself behind the nearest bushes to remove her skirt and replace it with a pair of trousers. Her voice came from the shrubbery, and she sounded troubled.

'Now see here, Mrs Reverend, I'm used to roughin' it, an' I don't mind ridin' all over the west with you in a buckboard, but I don't rightly see the purpose of it all. This sort of life ain't what my friends expected when they left me at your house!'

'But I've told you, Mrs Drummond, the Reverend travels an awful lot. I had that message he wanted certain things, an' I thought it would do you good to come out for a while instead of mopin' back there at my house. Besides, there's things I ain't told you yet, not wantin' to upset you followin' your recent troubles.'

Mirabelle came out from the bushes with her hat behind her neck, a stray lock of hair trailing across her face, and tucking in her shirt.

'You intrigue me, Mrs Reverend. I think I'm tougher than you give me credit for. So why don't you say what else you have in mind now before the coffee is ready?'

The older woman eyed her shrewdly. 'All righty, Missus Drummond, if that's the way you want it. It was lucky you came to our house an' not to anyone else's. You see, my husband was the man who married you. He knows more about your dead husband than a lot of people would give him credit for. He knows enough to believe that you might be in some sort of danger from your late husband's associates. When you have *that* kind of trouble, an ex-deputy ain't always the best kind of protection. So you see, you're in good hands out here with me, an' your welfare is bein' taken care of. Now, do you understand?'

'If your husband knew all this, why didn't you tell me earlier?' Mirabelle protested. These revelations had moved her rather deeply.

Her mind flitted back to Gorge City over the Colorado border where she had married Ben. She thought it was a coincidence that the same parson should be located in Studley, and that he should have the same name of Studley, too. Mirabelle had learned about the parson's surname from another paying guest at the house, but she saw nothing sinister in it at the time.

The older woman spread her hands. 'Didn't I jest give you a first-class excuse for that? On account of your bereavement an' all? Now come an' take your coffee an' stop botherin' that pretty head of yours with other folk's problems.'

Mirabelle shrugged rather prettily. She stuck a hand on her hip and patiently accepted a mug of coffee. 'Tell me, has your husband still got the beard? An' why didn't I remember his name was Studley, the same name as the town?'

Mrs Reverend started to fumble with a necklace tightly drawn about her neck. 'Oh, he shaved off his beard years ago, as soon as he thought his years were beginning to show on him. An' as for you not rememberin' his name, who can explain that? Some names stick an' others don't. Is the coffee to your likin'?'

Mirabelle nodded and smiled. She went off to see how the shaft horses were making out.

★ ★ ★

About a mile and a half farther south than the buckboard and the railroad track, the Reverend Studley was standing rather uncertainly on the trail proper, east of Studley by a mile or so. He was fingering the broad chin which had once worn a beard, and going over his detailed plans for what he intended to help happen in the next few hours.

In appearance, the parson was a little under average height. At fifty-six years of age he was a determined character with thick dark brows, steel-rimmed spectacles and a scrawny neck encircled with a soiled white clerical collar. His head was shaded by a big flat

Quaker-style hat and a black frockcoat enveloped his body. A gunbelt was partly hidden by his buttoned vest. The holster was farther back than most revolvers users would have it.

He glanced back into a tree clump where he had hidden his riding horse and wondered if it would be noticed when the stagecoach came along. He decided that it was safely hidden, and as the coach's approach had already been detected, he rubbed trail dust over his boots and the cuffs of his trousers and adopted the pose of a disgruntled man, long without use of his mount.

★ ★ ★

Fanner Kilrain, the coach driver, and his shotgun partner, Sam Baxter, were hand-picked for the tricky job of crewing the coach for the double journey. Fanner's right shoulder was lower than the other, a deformity he had suffered since birth. He used his right hand in the unusual cross-draw of

238

his gun, known as fanning, and thus made something of his peculiarity.

Sam Baxter, at forty-four, was a few years older, although he did not look it. He was a hard-faced Australian with big ears and nose and a thin, hard mouth. He liked people to know his nationality without asking. A bush hat, folded up at one side, underlined the impression given by his accent.

Sam was the first to speak as they rounded a certain bend. 'Hey, Fanner, will you tell me if my eyes have finally gone back on me? Is that, or is it not the reverend parson hombre out of Freighter's Ford?'

Fanner blinked hard. 'I get exactly the same impression, pardner, so it must be the parson. He sure is one kind of hombre hard to get rid of an' we don't want company on this trip, no sir.'

The Reverend Studley planted himself directly in the path of the coach horses and waved his arms in the air. He gave the impression of being exhausted and delighted to meet them. As Fanner made a half-hearted attempt to take the team around the parson, Studley shifted his footing with a great show of alacrity.

'You'll have to give in,' Sam whispered. 'He's determined.'

The coach stopped, and before Studley could get a word out, Fanner said his piece. 'Howdy Reverend, it sure is good to see you like always, but we can't take you aboard because this is an unscheduled trip an' we ain't allowed to take on passengers.'

'Regulations, young fellow. You shouldn't worry about such things at your age. It was unscheduled when my hoss tripped over a rattler an' then made off without me. I didn't ask to be left here in the way of your coach. So don't regard me as an ordinary passenger, eh? Jest give me a lift to wherever you're goin' an' leave the explainin' to yours truly!'

The pedestrian then scrambled on board.

16

Deputy Joe Lumb erupted into the camp of Sheriff Wagoner about half a mile west of the mine basin. He pulled up, looked around him and quickly surrendered his second, trailing horse when he perceived whose company he was in.

Joe was not a man to smile very often, but his mouth quirked when Scott Wagoner rose from a fallen tree and crossed to shake his hand.

'I know you. You must be Joe, Ira Lumb's nephew. But what is it, Joe? Do you have special news for me?'

The newcomer began: 'My uncle sent me. On account of your ex-deputy, Jeff Mays, comin' into the office with Red Richards an' Mr Jasen, the manager of the big bank.' He paused for breath and then recounted what had happened, putting in all that Jeff had said about

241

the payroll's progress and the possible routes which the robbers might take, in the event that they struck before the mine was reached.

Wagoner slapped his weak thigh. 'That boy Jeff sure is keyed up an' in touch.' He glanced round his force and beckoned Rex Burgh towards him. 'Rex, I want you to pick two of the best mounted men in this outfit, an' ride with them a few points east of north. You'll strike the main trail east out of Studley. Get into cover an' look out for an ordinary stagecoach. If it's gone through, follow it an' bring it to a stop until I get there. If it hasn't reached that point, still stop it and hold the crew. You see, the point is, it ought to be comin' directly here, bringing a big payroll. You understand, Rex?'

Burgh nodded solemnly. His dark eyes flashed. Here was the sheriff at last recognising his undoubted ability. It felt good. As he was striding off to pick his two riding partners, Wagoner called after him: 'Me an' the rest of the boys will be movin' over on to the mine approach track an' ridin' up it until we locate that same coach, an' anybody who's been near it for the wrong sort of reasons. All right?'

Burgh signalled with his hand. Two men who had also caught the action fever, readily agreed to go with Burgh. They mounted up in a hurry and rode off towards the mine track, which they would cross on their way to their approved observation spot.

Wagoner cleared his throat. 'To your horses, boys!'

Deputy Lumb was with them as they found the track and moved north.

★ ★ ★

A mile further east than the place where Studley had stopped the coach for a lift eight outlaws were patiently waiting behind a straight line of boulders which jutted out of the hillside on the northern fringe of the trail. At the back of the rock line, the earth had been hollowed out so that men within a hundred and fifty feet of the trail could walk about upright, unseen from below, and also hide their horses, which were in a state of readiness for a quick move.

Numbered among the active eight members of the Yerby gang were Jinx Farrimond, Lon Birk, Lofty Rington and Jack Whale. Men known as Slim, Curly and Pecos made up the number of those who took orders. The current leader of the gang, the man who implemented the boss's orders, was also there. His name was Rock Grant. Grant had been actively breaking the law for more than half of his thirty-nine years. He had a thick, barrel chest; a full, grim, cleanshaven face always tinted with the blue-black colour of his hair; and a pair of flinty eyes which always looked mildly forbidding on account of a slight squint.

Jinx Farrimond took his eye away from the glass he was holding and glanced in Grant's direction.

'Here comes the coach, right now,

Rock!' He shouted, spluttering in his excitement. 'You want to take a look?'

Grant yawned and tugged at the lobe of an ear. 'All right, let me see!'

He took the glass, rested it on top of a rock and panned it as the horse-drawn vehicle slowly came nearer, turning up dust with its wheels. He consulted a pocket watch and decided that everything was going as planned. Abruptly he snapped the glass shut, and turned to give orders.

'Lon, you know the exact spot you have to be at beside the trail?'

Birk nodded and started towards his horse.

'Make sure you don't make any unnecessary noise on the way down there, then!' Grant called after him. He detailed off Farrimond, Whale and Rington to go along with Birk, and then turned his attention back to the trail.

Presently, he gave the orders to evacuate the observation point.

Meanwhile, Parson Studley was also thinking about the time. He started to put into play an act which had to pay off in a certain time. Squatting on the back seat, opposite the flap through which the crew could see him, he began to crouch over his knees.

He waited for a suitable time when the coach was making the least noise, and then conjured up a most heart-rending moan. Sam Baxter glanced through the small aperture and saw him doubled up over one knee. 'What in tarnation is the matter, Reverend? Are you sick, or somethin'?'

'Not sick, my man, jest in the foul grip of the greatest pain that ever attacks me! It's cramp! Every now an' again I get this awful cramp. The muscles in my leg lock, an' I can't shift myself for hours. Mostly I come out in a cold sweat, an' then lose consciousness!'

Baxter withdrew his head and exchanged a significant glance with Fanner. He did not know whether secretly to make fun of the parson's malady, or whether to feel sorry for him. All he usually concerned himself over was the breaking of the special bank regulations about taking on unwarranted passengers and being lured down off the box.

The Australian murmured: 'Well, what do you think, pardner?'

Before Fanner could reply, Studley had a loud suggestion to make. 'Say, if you fellows could slow down long enough for the guard to come in here an' give me a hand, I'd be over this in no time at all. What do you say, seein' you haven't any scheduled passengers on board?'

It was Kilrain's turn to hesitate. 'I wouldn't want you to think we're indifferent to your sufferin', Reverend — '

'Ah! I think this is the worst attack I've had all this year,' Studley bellowed, in a much louder voice. 'Say, are you goin' to slow this coach or do I have to go on sufferin'?'

With a great sigh, Fanner gave in. He slowed the horses to a walk, nodded to

Baxter, and watched the latter drop down to trail level and swing open the coach door on the side facing north. Baxter disappeared into the seating space. Studley, still bent double, gestured for Baxter to bend down beside him and take a hand. As soon as the Australian had laid aside his bush hat, he crouched over the locked limb and glanced up for direction as to where he should apply pressure, or alternatively, massage.

In that instant, Studley crooked an arm round his neck, holding him in a grip like a vice. The other hand, hidden from the aperture by their two bodies, came up with a long, thin-bladed knife in it. The point of the blade pricked the skin of Baxter's neck. Perspiration shot out of his pores and bathed him within seconds.

Studley turned the blade. It was one he had sharpened and ground himself for no other purpose. 'Listen an' listen good, Aussie. I want you to call out to the driver to stop the coach an' come down to help you. Tell him it'll save a lot of time in the end. Insist if you have to, an' don't do anythin' to make me nervous.'

One of Baxter's eyelids started to twitch. Studley prompted him to get a move on.

'Fanner! Can you hear me, Fanner?'

Having said this, his throat dried. There was little wonder over that. Studley cautiously studied the aperture and what the driver would see when he glanced down. He was satisfied.

'You callin', Sam?' A brief look and then the driver looked away again.

'Yer, I was, Fanner. I want you to stop the coach an' come on in 'ere to give us a 'and. The Reverend's in worse trouble than we thought!'

'Are you sure you can't manage without that?' Fanner protested.

He did not trouble to look that time, and when Sam finally implored him to come straight away, he reined in the horses and braked. By that time, Baxter was breathing more easily, although he had no idea of the outcome of this sudden threat by a man of the cloth.

Studley's face was very close to Baxter's as the knife was slowly removed from the neck and shifted to a lower target. Before the Australian had adjusted to the new threat, the blade had entered his ribs at the front and pierced his heart.

Holding him in a grip of iron, Studley jerked the blade a second time and then slowly withdrew it.

Kilrain's puzzled countenance showed at the window. His lined face showed his bewilderment as he peered down at the two bodies and tried to make out who was ministering to whom.

'Come on in, Fanner, we need you,' Studley panted. 'Here, bend over here!'

Kilrain briefly rocked the coach as he moved into it. He pushed back his hat, rubbed his face with his bandanna and crouched over the other pair. Studley worked the knife around the corpse of his first victim and administered a death blow to Fanner, aiming an upwards swing which landed in the driver's chest in the same area as before.

Kilrain gasped. He lowered his hands, set his teeth and appeared to rise on the end of the knife. He managed to murmur the name of his dead comrade, and then he was toppling over Baxter's lifeless body, partly on the floor and partly propped on the seat.

One of them emitted a death rattle as the killer scrambled clear. It gave him no cause for concern, as death was scarcely unknown to him. After cautiously looking up and down the trail, Studley got out, closed the door and clambered up on to the box, breathing hard. He kicked off the brake and started the vehicle in motion.

His spectacles had fogged up in the brief struggle. He pulled them off and cleaned them on a handkerchief. After that, he gave his full attention to the route, and he did not pause again until he had reached a predetermined spot. There, he stopped the vehicle, consulted his gold hunter watch, and proceeded to haul the two bodies out of the seating area. He dumped them on the trail, and straightened up.

Hands on hips, he glared at the nearest bit of concealing foliage fifteen yards away. 'All right, I know you're there. What are you waitin' for? Get round to the boot and haul out the payroll! You can get these bodies into cover later. Do I have to tell you to hurry?'

Lon Birk led the rush for the boot, closely followed by Farrimond, Whale and Rington, all of whom showed a macabre interest in the dead crew members. A leather satchel holding dollar bills and a metal box containing coin were quickly hoisted out of the luggage section and taken off trail.

Jinx was about to pick up the guard when his ears detected something.

'Hosses comin' up fast from the rear, Reverend!'

Studley swore a round oath. He listened and decided that time was short. 'All right, get out of sight with that money! Rock knows the drill! We'll have to leave the bodies! Get goin'!'

Studley had the coach going forward again as if he had driven it all his life. The vehicle rocked.

17

Birk and Farrimond, who were perhaps the most responsible of the present crew, used a few precious seconds to drag Kilrain and Baxter to the side of the trail before they plunged into scrub cover and went for their horses. Whale and Rington were holding the spare horses and keenly anxious to move off when they reached the tethering spot.

'All right, let's go,' Birk suggested.

He was almost jostled off the track, so keen were the others.

Jeff and Red would most probably have gone past the place where the unloading had happened if the buckskin had not galloped near the body of one of the dead and scared itself. Jeff called out, and Red circled the spot, all the time watching out in case of shooting from the ample cover in the area. They thought they heard the sound of retreating riders, but they could not be sure. The rustling leaves covered most small sounds.

'Our best move is still to follow the coach. After all, it ain't here, an' somebody's drivin' it!' Jeff pointed out.

'What are we waitin' for?' Red enquired, as his sorrel shot ahead.

Once again they rode flat out with the breeze buffeting their bodies and their mounts. The minutes slipped by. Ahead of them they heard sounds which suggested the coach was being driven along at a furious pace. From time to time, the partners glanced across at one another. The fury of the pace could not be kept up indefinitely. Some new development had to occur, if they were not to fall out of the race because of their horses' tiredness.

The gradient changed slightly about every hundred yards; so did the direction. A great distance seemed to have gone by when the trail began to move upgrade, slowly straightening itself out.

'I think we must be comin' to the fork in the trail,' Jeff yelled hoarsely.

'Yer,' Red returned, 'we'll soon know. Whichever way the coach goes, I'd still gamble the man on the box is an outlaw, though!'

Jeff was unshaken in the same view. They were gaining, but slowly. The dust put up by the coach's wheels and the team's hooves seemed to hang higher and even to taste differently. The mine fork came up on their right, drawing their attention for a short time.

Suddenly they became aware of pounding hooves almost on a parallel course with them, off to the south. Jeff pointed, and they slowed for a while, peering round cautiously in case they were about to contact more renegades. Out from the trees and on to the mine track came Major Dunlap and his tiring riders. They pulled up in a body as the coach pursuers altered course and paused to speak to them.

'Major, I'm glad you made it to

here!' Jeff gasped, forgetting his previous dislike of the ex-military man. 'The coach has gone on, some renegade is almost certainly in charge of it. If your men don't mind more ridin', members of the raidin' gang are in the hilly patch of country between the trail and the railroad. The place where they left the trail was probably two miles back. You can locate it again because the driver an' the guard of the stagecoach are lyin' dead beside the spot! How do you feel about goin' after them?'

The Major backed his horse. His men were crowding him on all sides.

He put forward one argument. 'Shouldn't we tackle the coach first?'

'I don't think so,' Jeff argued back. 'The sheriff will almost certainly have sent men up that stretch of trail, to cover such an eventuality as we have now. Besides, Red, here, an' I, we can tackle whoever is drivin'! More personnel would be wasted, I think!'

'Very well, Mays, we'll be advised by you!' The Major saluted and indicated that his men were to follow him. Looking rather down in the mouth, they went off down the trail towards Studley, sniffing at the dust which would remain with them until they came to the bodies.

Just as the buckskin and the sorrel were circling and about to go off on the interrupted pursuit, the sound of a rifle being fired carried back to them. Jeff grinned. There was confirmation that the sheriff had posted men in the eastern section of the trail.

'Come on, pardner,' Red called, 'there might still be work for us to do!'

A volley of revolver fire came next, and then more shots from two rifles. The echoes gradually got farther away, and the pursuing pair of riders slowed as they reached the scene of the exchanges.

Rex Burgh, who was having trouble in getting his horse under control, stepped to the side of the trail with one of his men.

'Careful how you go when you catch

up with the coach. It's a parson up on the box, an' he's already killed one deputy! We'll be after you as soon as we can make it!'

The pursuers waved and called back an acknowledgement of the message. Each of them then knew that the Reverend Studley was the villain of this latest Yerby piece. Probably he had killed the coach crew, as well as the man he had just shot. Jeff wondered how and why a man of the cloth had slipped off the straight and narrow road, and joined the brethren of the owlhoot trail. The conjecture was pushed aside as they caught their first glimpse of the speeding coach.

Red sighted it, swinging on its leather straps. Jeff then spotted the crouching figure perched on the box, flailing the horses' backs with the whip. The driver caught sight of them at the same time, giving them a long glance through his thick spectacles. He appeared to come to some decision.

For a time, they gained at a greater

speed. That was before the shotgun was discharged in their direction, and then the brace of revolvers. A lucky shot could have winged them, but none did. Even so, there were bullets which passed within a foot of horse or rider.

Studley emptied two revolvers, as well as the shotgun. He then turned to a lightweight rifle, with which he seemed much more formidable. His shots were infrequent, but they went closer. The distance between coach and pursuit was no more than forty yards when Jeff unsheathed his Winchester and began to return the fire.

Red, a side-iron marksman, held off and watched him. Four shots, at even intervals, all missed before the fifth — a lucky one — hit the reverend gentleman in the head and spilled him in slow motion towards the dirt of the trail . . .

He was dead when they approached his crumpled, hatless body.

After that, it was a search for the buckboard, which Jeff felt certain was supposed to contact the lone clergy-man. Keeping their mounts at a walking pace, they crossed intervening ground between trail and rail track and settled to rest on high ground not far from the permanent way.

Their fire showed for quite a distance, especially as the light began to fail. It was almost dusk when Red's glass picked up the image of the missing buckboard moving slowly along from the west. He passed it to Jeff, who confirmed to his own satisfaction that he was seeing Mrs Reverend and Mirabelle, and that the latter did not appear to be harmed in any way.

'I'm sure Mrs Reverend is involved in her husband's illegal acts, Red,' Jeff stated, 'but we may have to play out this little scene with tact. Maybe you should leave the talkin' to me.'

They clambered down off their perch and went to meet the buckboard, showing the parson's wife every cour-tesy. When all were seated by the fire, and the old woman was explaining that her husband had not appeared where he said he would be, Jeff took it upon himself to make an explanation.

'Mrs Reverend, we know more about your husband's recent movements than you do. As a matter of fact, he's had an accident on trail. A fatal one connected with a stagecoach. I'm sorry to be the bearer of bad news. Maybe we can locate his body in the daylight.'

The woman seemed stunned, but the firelight reflected enough animation in her face to show that her brain was busy. When the time came to retire, Jeff felt more uneasy than on any night since the recent disturbances began. Mirabelle and the Studley widow slept a little way back on one side of the fire, while the men curled up diagonally opposite.

Around two in the morning, the older woman startled a sleeping camp when she appeared beside the fire and clicked the bolt on a rifle. Her first bullet ploughed into the saddle on which Jeff's head was resting. He moved, and Red slithered away, but it was a six-gun fired by Mirabelle which put an end to the shooting. The bullet glanced off the rifle and struck the old woman in the heart. She swayed, and eventually fell, having confirmed that on occasion she could be as vicious as her husband.

The girl who might have been used as a hostage dropped her gun and ran to the men for comfort.

★　★　★

The bank guards and the sheriff's posse between them finished off the so-called Yerby gang which had been run by the Reverend Studley for a long time. Farrimond and Whale were captured and went to the penitentiary; all the rest were killed except a Mexican named Pecos, who set off for the Mexican border early and made it ahead of pursuit.

The payroll money was recovered and returned to the mine.

When Jeff, Mirabelle and Red reached Studley the following day, Sheriff Wagoner had just announced that he was about to retire. He made it clear that he wanted Jeff as his successor, and Jeff said he would consider the appointment provided his partner, Red Richards, could take on as chief deputy.

Red startled the occupants of the marshal's office by putting in a word of his own. 'Ain't nobody asked me this far,' he grumbled, 'but I might take such a job in the event of a certain lady of my kin settles in the county seat.'

'An' what do *you* say about it, Mirabelle?' Wagoner asked.

The Widow Drummond winked and smiled. 'Ask me again when we get back home,' was all she would say.